FOREVER - BOOK 1

Forever Now

elise sax

Cover design: Elizabeth Mackey

EliseSax.com

EliseSax@gmail.com

http://elisesax.com/mailing-list.php

https://www.facebook.com/ei.sax.9

@TheEliseSax

ISBN: 1505635349
ISBN-13: 978-1505635348

Also by Elise Sax

The Matchmaker Series

An Affair to Dismember

Matchpoint

Love Game

Field of Screams

Wish Upon A Stud Series

Going Down

Man Candy

Hot Wired

Just Sacked

Wicked Ride

Bounty

Switched

Moving Violations

For Luis

Chapter 1

Forever is composed of nows.

--Emily Dickinson

What would Emily Dickinson do? Since she never left her room, writing poetry while stuffed in a high-necked corseted dress, I don't think she would go out like *this.*

Like … ugh. Blech.

This.

I threw a sweater over my mirror. I couldn't bear to look at my body parts oozing out of the bikini my mom bought me. I mean, made me wear. I mean, threatened me if I didn't wear it at her pool party.

Pool parties. I bet Emily Dickinson never had to go to a pool party.

I poked my stomach, which pooched out below my belly button, on full display in the white bathing suit. I tried to suck in my pooch, but that's when I noticed the mushy part pushing against the side strap of my bikini bottoms. It was like my butt had infiltrated my hip.

I had side butt.

I crawled into bed and pulled the covers over my head. It felt good to hide. Maybe my mom would think I left town, I hoped. I had Pop Tarts stashed in my nightstand, so I could last a couple days hidden like that in my room. Well, a day and a half—I really liked Pop Tarts.

It was as good a plan as any.

No matter what, there was no way I was going downstairs dressed in a tiny white bikini. No way. NO. WAY. My mom could drag me out by my fingernails and I wouldn't go. She could take away the television and waterboard me, and I wouldn't go.

My bedroom door swung open and banged into the wall. "What the hell!" my mom screeched.

I stopped breathing. I didn't move a muscle. I stayed under the covers and thought invisible thoughts. That is, I tried to be invisible, which really wasn't hard, normally. I had been basically invisible for sixteen years, which was my entire life.

"I'm not a moron," Mom yelled. "I know you're hiding under the covers. You're not exactly flat as a pancake, you know."

Ouch. When she wasn't ignoring me, my mother was good at being mean.

Although lately, she wasn't her normal ogre self. She had spent the morning dancing around the house in her bikini, putting up streamers, and setting up the blender to make endless margaritas for her guests. She was in her happy mood, her usual mood when she found a new boyfriend. Mom went through boyfriends like I went through ninety-nine-cent notebooks.

And I went through a lot of ninety-nine-cent notebooks. You see, I was a writer, or wanted to be a writer. In fact, I wanted to study writing in Paris like Hemingway and Gertrude Stein. But since I was an invisible girl in San Diego with a bunch of cheap notebooks and Bic pens, I had no chance of ever making it to France. I was going to have to continue to be Emily Dickinson it in my room by myself. I mean, write in my notebooks that nobody would ever see until way after I was dead…which hopefully would be before I had to traipse downstairs in the white bikini that showed too much extra me.

I was going to start my senior year in a month without hope of ever seeing the Eiffel Tower. Instead of the Sorbonne, I was most likely only going to see the local community college and a would-you-like-fries-with-that-job after I graduated.

In the meantime, I just had to get through Mom and her never-ending supply of new boyfriends. Although, this one was supposed to be different. This one was supposed to be *the one.*

"Don't screw this up for me," she ordered, pulling the blankets off my face. "You'll come down for at least an hour and act like you're happy to see him. If I see that sour puss on your face, I'm going to slap it off."

My mother had slapped the sour puss off my face twice before. So I knew she was serious. Still, I didn't want to be anywhere near her boyfriends and even less at her pool party, which would be filled with her drunk friends from her work and from the bar she liked to hang out at in the evenings.

"You might have some fun," my mom added. "Put on that

nice bathing suit I bought you, and for the love of God, no hats."

She yanked my sweater off the mirror and checked herself out. She was four inches shorter than my five-foot-seven, a tiny little woman with a tiny little body topped with a tiny little nose and long, silky smooth blond hair. She was wearing a white bikini, too, but there were no extra bits sticking out. No pooch.

No side butt.

I hated that she had bought me the bikini. She would skin me alive if I didn't wear it. My mother usually forgot that I needed stuff like clothes and shoes for school and then all of a sudden she would buy me something like a bikini, even though I didn't inherit her bikini body, or earrings, even though my ears weren't pierced.

My mom checked out her makeup in the mirror one more time and skipped out of the room. New boyfriends sure made her happy.

I started to sweat and kicked off my covers. I couldn't figure out how to get out of the party and my walk of shame. I didn't think my mother would fall for an Ebola excuse. Thankfully, I stumbled on a technicality. I had to wear the bikini, but I could wear something *over* it.

I had just the right t-shirt. It said *Moe's Tires* and hung to right above my knees. I slipped it over my head and took a look in the mirror. Perfect. For the first time all day, I was happy, just like I had a new boyfriend. It's funny what a large swathe of cotton can do for morale.

I was tempted by the hat, hanging on the back of my

bedroom door, even though Mom would blow a gasket if I wore it. The hat was wide-brimmed and made of straw, and I felt like a movie star in it. I had bought it with my babysitting money, which I usually saved to buy milk, cereal, and peanut butter when my mother forgot to buy food.

I decided that hats were *me.* And since there wasn't much me in the world—I was invisible, remember—I didn't think there was much harm in a couple of floppy hats. My mom didn't agree, and she didn't let me wear them anywhere near her, especially when The Boyfriend was around.

According to my mom, I didn't know how to act around boyfriends, and maybe she was right. I had never had a boyfriend. Not even close. I mean, if you don't count Jerry Katz in third grade, who tried to marry me during recess. I said no, and he moved on to Tiffany Banks by the end of the day.

Boys. Who needs 'em?

I pulled my long brown hair into a ponytail, left the hat on the door, and walked downstairs just in time to see my mom in a lip-lock with her new boyfriend.

Okay, here's the thing. Once, when I was eight years old, I heard my only friend's mother tell another woman that I was "neglected." I tucked the word away until the next day at school when I looked it up in the dictionary.

Neglected: disregarded; lacking a caretaker.

My mom went through long patches of time where she forgot that I existed, and it usually happened when she got a new boyfriend. So, I was the kid who walked herself to kindergarten, and I was the kid who ate Skittles and Hershey bars for lunch every day until the lunch ladies got me on free lunch. And free breakfast.

Because I was neglected, because I had no parental supervision, parents wouldn't let their kids play with me, and I got used to being alone. Because I was neglected, I called 911 the first time I got my period.

But being neglected isn't the worst thing about having a mom with lots of boyfriends.

Going downstairs and seeing her in a lip-lock is the worst thing about having a mom with lots of boyfriends.

Her newest boyfriend—*The Boyfriend*--was tall and handsome (she said) with one of those beards that looked like he forgot to shave that morning. He was half-French and half-Puerto Rican and had traveled everywhere. He insisted that Mom throw out all of our frozen food and forced me to eat disgusting stuff like paella. He also loved wine and always brought a bottle to the house when he visited.

In fact, he had a bottle in his hand while he stuck his tongue down my mom's throat. I wondered if he had a whole supply of wine in the trunk of his car or something.

It went on for a while. There were even moaning and sucking sounds. I looked at the clock on the entrance way wall. I had fifty-five minutes to go before I would be allowed to return to my room. Fifty-five minutes can take a long time.

"I told you to put on the bathing suit!" My mom

screeched, pulling away from The Boyfriend's lips with a smacking sound. "I paid good money for that!"

I jumped back in surprise and embarrassment. Mom went from gross kisser to seething screamer in a split second. She stared me down, her chest heaving with anger.

Some of the party guests peeked their heads into the entrance way to see what made my mom yell, and The Boyfriend looked at me like I was the mosquito who wouldn't stop buzzing around his head.

I shrank to nothing. It was like *Honey, I Shrunk the Kids,* but I was even smaller. Humiliated small. Mortified small.

But not small enough.

I closed my eyes and willed myself to disappear. *Anywhere but here*, I wished. Anywhere. Prison. Somalia. Math class.

"It's under the shirt," I said, my voice coming out all croaky and quiet. I could feel my face go red. I was a terrible blusher.

I looked back at the clock. Fifty-three minutes to go.

"Laura," The Boyfriend said to her, changing the subject. "Let me introduce you to my son, Cruz."

Like magic, the attention turned away from me and my humiliation to The Boyfriend's son. Mom and her already half-drunk guests stared him down with appreciation.

I don't know why I didn't notice him before because he

was the best looking boy I had ever seen. Not really a boy. A man. Maybe nineteen, I figured. He had dark hair and eyes but light skin, and he was tall and muscular. He was beautiful, like a model, shining under the lights.

Perfect.

He shook my mother's hand, and the three of them walked on the tiled floor further into the house without saying a word to me.

Invisible.

There. That's the moment my life changed. No, I didn't realize it, yet. I didn't know that anything special had happened. I certainly didn't know that Cruz would save my life, and I would save his—at least for a while. That we would love each other and our love would be dangerous.

Chapter 2

The soul should always stand ajar, ready to welcome the ecstatic experience.

--Emily Dickinson

Blaring. Ear-splitting. Nauseating.

Disco.

The music that had announced wide-collared, all-rayon shirts, and man perms forty years ago was blasting from the living room. My house had gone back in time to 1977, and the Bee Gees were singing all about it at the top of their lungs in a falsetto that sounded like Mariah Carey and made me giggle.

Hyper-happy, bikini-clad Mom danced with The Boyfriend, barefoot on the shag carpet in the living room. They swirled around like two old farts and occasionally bumping into the couch and the recliner. The guests stood by, holding drinks and watching the dancing.

I wanted to vomit.

And kill myself.

And point and laugh.

My mom had ordered me to make margaritas in the kitchen, and I was more than happy to do it. Anything not to watch them.

But I had a problem. I couldn't make margaritas because Cruz was sitting at the kitchen counter, his arms resting only inches away from the blender. I couldn't handle the blender without touching him, and if I touched him, I would wind up jumping on his back and licking him from his head to his toes.

That might be embarrassing.

I hovered at the kitchen entrance, debating with myself about what to do. If I didn't make the margaritas, my mother would literally kill me, but I didn't want to be known as "the licker." Stuff like that gets around, and being invisible was bad enough. I didn't want to add, "The licker" to my list of miseries.

I knocked on the side of my head. What was wrong with me? What was I scared of? How likely was it that I was going to lick a perfect stranger?

Who was I kidding? It was ninety-nine percent sure I would lick him. Cruz looked yummier than cookie dough ice cream, and he smelled yummy, too. I was getting a good whiff of him from my position in the kitchen, and his odor was making me dizzy.

I caught myself licking my lips, and I stuck my tongue back in my mouth. The music changed from the Bee Gees to Donna Summer. I heard the dancers bump into the wall. They would be wanting more drinks soon.

I didn't have long before my mother would start screaming

at me for not making the drinks fast enough, and maybe this time, she would insist I take my t-shirt off. I would be a lot better off if I made the margaritas quickly and got out of my mom's line of sight.

But I couldn't move from my spot. It was a really, really good vantage point, there between the toaster and the refrigerator. I could see all of Cruz. His perfect, sculpted cheekbones. His big round, brown eyes, fringed in long black eyelashes. His hair.

Oh, his thick, beautiful, lickable hair.

And then there was his body, sitting on the barstool, his feet tucked underneath him, his muscular thighs poking out from under his bathing suit. His muscly, long, beautiful body.

Like Lot's wife turning back, I had to look at him. Looking at him was a pleasure, like eating ice cream on a hot day, or slipping into a warm bath to soothe sore muscles.

I could stare at him all I wanted, because he was too busy looking at his hands to notice. It dawned on me that he didn't want to watch the dancing any more than I did, and that made me indescribably happy.

Not that I thought I had any chance with him. I was the invisible girl. He hadn't even said hello to me, even though we were the only two people in the kitchen.

I loved to look at him. That was enough for me. He was beautiful. Special. I felt a flutter of happiness, as my eyes traveled from his face to his muscular shoulders, which were on display in his blue tank top.

Muscle T, I thought. That's what it's called. Of course he would wear something with *muscle* in the name. It fit him.

I had a terrible desire to write in my notebook. I could write pages and pages about his shoulders. Wide and tan, muscly but not bodybuilder big. *Cut.* That's what he was. I tapped my forehead to pound the memory of him into my brain. I would have to note every detail and save it for always. That way, I could look at him forever.

My eyes darted to the digital clock on the microwave. Forty-eight minutes to go before I could return to my room and write about Cruz.

The beginning of a story was taking form in my mind. In it, I would call Cruz, Roman, and he would be a prince and save a girl from kidnappers—No, a tsunami!—and her name would be Emma or Olivia. No…Pippa!

While I hashed out the story in my head, I assembled the ingredients for the margaritas and placed them on the counter at a safe distance from Cruz's arms. Then, it was the moment of truth. I took the lid off the blender and put it down on the marbled granite, almost grazing his fingertips.

Cruz's hands flew off the counter, presumably to not touch me. Our eyes locked for the briefest of moments. His look drew me into him, like Alice down the rabbit hole. Down, down, down I fell into another world.

Lost.

My ears grew hot, and my breath hitched. An electrical charge ran through my body—the after effects of our connection, like I had put my finger in a socket. Or worse.

The room spun around, and I took a step back, trying to catch my balance.

Off with her head, I thought, dimly.

I felt like Cruz had tried to communicate something in that moment, but I didn't understand the language of boys, and I couldn't ask him because the moment had gone. And because I would never talk to him. Never. Was this what *boy crazy* was? Had I gone crazy at the sight of a perfect boy? Is this what happened to Angelina Jolie when she met Brad Pitt?

Of course not. Cruz was much better looking than Brad Pitt.

I took a healing breath and went back to looking at him. With his hands now in his lap, he studied them even more intently.

My mouth had dropped open, and I closed it. Then, I remembered to blink. What was I supposed to be doing before Cruz rearranged my molecules with a split-second look? Oh, yes.

I poured margarita mix, tequila, and ice into the blender, sneaking glances at Cruz the whole time. I forgot about my made-up story, too intent at looking at the real thing.

I followed the line of his muscles down his arms to his hands. Strong. I had never studied a boy before. I had never looked too closely. It was better than the books described.

Then, it wasn't better. In fact, it was pretty miserable. In the books, the boy looked back. In the books, the goo-goo eyes went both ways. I needed another connection and quick. I wanted more Alice down the rabbit hole. I wanted more electrical charge.

I wanted Cruz to see me.

I didn't want to be invisible.

Donna Summer ended her song with a long, four-on-the-floor beat, and I could hear my mom and The Boyfriend stumble out of the living room.

"Uh oh," I said and slapped on the lid and switched the *on* switch. It made a horrible grinding noise. I prayed I had put in the right amounts of margarita mix and tequila, but luckily, my mother and her guests were already halfway to sloshed and wouldn't notice if the recipe was slightly off.

I finished just as she stepped into the kitchen, clinging to The Boyfriend with her guests trailing behind her. I backed away from the blender and skulked into the corner.

Forty-three minutes until I could go upstairs.

"Get the cups, Tess," Mom ordered me. "The red plastic ones."

Cruz's head snapped up, and he looked at me like I had sprouted a couple more ears. I shuddered and tried to get my hands to work. Luckily, the fear of my mother was stronger than anything Cruz could inflict through his dreamy eyes.

I handed her the cups, and she poured drinks.

"How are you getting on?" The Boyfriend asked Cruz.

"Fine," he said. Cruz's voice was deep and soft. I could have listened to it forever.

"Feel free to use the pool whenever you want," Mom sing-songed to him and gulped down a margarita like it was a 7Up.

"Thanks," he said. "You want to?"

The second part—the question part—was directed to me. He was looking right at me, smiling, and asking me something. I willed my mouth to work.

"Uh—" I said, finally.

Dumb. Dumb. Dumb. Emily Dickinson wasn't dumb. Why did I have to be dumb? Why couldn't I say something meaningful and funny? Something smart?

I cleared my throat and started again. "What?" I asked.

Dumb.

"Come on. Let's go," he said, putting his hand out to me.

The world stopped spinning on its axis. The tides rolled backwards, and birds fell from the sky.

Cruz's hand levitated in the air, outstretched, waiting, and his attention was on me and nobody else. I inhaled deeply and watched as my hand took on a life of its own and slipped into his. My fingers glided over his palm, and his hand closed over mine.

Found.

He hopped off the barstool and tugged me out of the

house.

"That's better," he said, once we were standing on the deck at the shallow end of the small pool. He pulled off his shirt and tossed it on a chair. My eyes teared up. It was like a Calvin Klein commercial had come to life minus the air brushing.

Cruz didn't need air brushing.

I pinched myself. For the first time in my life, everything was perfect. I hadn't even followed my bliss, but here it was in front of me, half-naked and sporting a six pack. No, an eight pack!

Bliss. Happiness.

And then just like that, it was over.

"You ready?" he asked. It was time for me to take off my shirt and reveal my side butt.

No way. No way. No. Way. I hated the bikini. I hated my side butt. How could I hide my side butt? Why was I cursed with side butt?

"Are you okay?" he asked. "You're kind of sweaty."

I had broken out into a huge sweat. My t-shirt was wet, and my hair had come undone from my ponytail and was sticking to my face in long, wet strips.

Eight packs had that effect on me. Also, he expected me to talk to him. He was actually paying attention to me. I didn't know what had changed. One minute I was invisible; the next minute, he was stripping down and wanting to swim with me.

Obviously, he didn't know about my side butt.

"After you," I said. "It takes me a long time to get undressed."

Dumb.

He shrugged his shoulders and stepped down into the pool. The minute he had his back turned, I ripped off my shirt and took a fast running jump into the water. I splashed down so fast that my side butt was only a blur.

Genius.

I tread water in the deep end, and Cruz breaststroked his way to me. "Nice," he said. "I give it a nine-point-seven. Point-three off for not tucking your knees in during the cannonball entry."

I spit out pool water like a fountain gnome. I still couldn't believe he was speaking to me.

"You're talking to me," I pointed out.

"Yeah, about that," he said. "Sorry I was giving you the cold shoulder. I thought you were Brooke Lyon, and I was a little star struck."

"Brooke Lyon the movie star?"

"I'm kind of shy."

"Brooke Lyon, the beautiful movie star?"

"Then, your mom called you Tess, and I realized my

mistake."

"Brooke Lyon, the beautiful movie star who was voted Best Dressed Hottie on the Red Carpet at the Emmys last year?"

"I know. Stupid," he said, shrugging. He waded to the side and held onto the wall. I followed him.

"Do you go to Hoover High?" he asked me.

I nodded. "Brooke Lyon the runner up for Sexiest Woman Alive in Maxim magazine?"

Either I had died and had gone to heaven, or I slipped through a wormhole into another dimension where I was a dead-ringer for Brooke Lyon. Since I wasn't particularly spiritual or a sci-fi freak, I was baffled.

"I'm going to go to Uni. It starts next week. My dad has a condo near there," he said. "My parents had a bad breakup. I'm trying life with my father for a while," he explained, freely telling me about his life.

He was a new kid. No wonder he was talking to me. He didn't know I was invisible, yet. I hoped he liked wine and paella because I didn't see a lot of Bagel Bites in his future.

"I thought you were older," I said.

"Eighteen. Senior."

I was sixteen and a senior, but I had skipped fifth grade, and I was turning seventeen in December.

"I'm a senior, too," I said.

"Cool."

Cool. I was cool. My high school status was cool. Side butt and everything...cool.

Maybe I was dead, after all.

We played together in the water for hours. We splashed each other, did three rounds of Marco Polo, and simulated water skiing where I stood on his bent legs, he held my hands, and ran around the shallow end.

Luckily, the water was cold enough that when I touched him, I didn't burst into flames.

When we were thoroughly pickled, we got out and sat by the umbrella-covered table on the deck. We ate something called hummus with kale chips. The Boyfriend had banished onion dip and Cheetos from our property.

Getting out of the pool without Cruz seeing my mostly nakedness was harder than going in. I actually did a "Look over there!" move. He was still looking over there when I wrapped myself in a big beach towel, safely on the deck.

"Where? Where? I still can't see the eagle," he said while we ate kale chips.

"It flew away."

We sat outside and talked until the disco music ended, until the sun went down, and the margaritas and beer were gone, taking the guests with them. We talked about TV and movies and kale chips. He talked about his goals in life—to be rich with a Tesla because it was sicker than a Maserati. My goals in life—Living in Paris, writing in my notebooks and miraculously sipping coffee with Hemingway, even though he had been dead for over a half of a century.

Cruz didn't care about Paris or Hemingway, but he had a lot to say about coffee, and we talked for another thirty minutes about lattes versus mochas before my mother slinked out of the house, hanging over The Boyfriend like he had sprouted a human cape.

I could smell the alcohol wafting out of her pores from twenty feet away. The Boyfriend didn't smell all that teetotalery either.

It had been magical, spending one-on-one time with Cruz. I didn't even mind the burning in my gut from the hummus and kale chips. But all good things must come to an end, and my good thing ended at 8:30 that Saturday night at the end of August.

The Boyfriend summoned Cruz, and after ten minutes of my mom saying goodbye in baby talk—*Will you miss me a widdle bit? I'm gonna miss wu!*—The Boyfriend and Cruz left.

No, he didn't ask me for my phone number. No, no plans to see me later.

Just a wave and a thousand-watt smile.

With mom's track record with men, she was sure to break up with The Boyfriend in a matter of minutes, and I would never see Cruz again.

As soon as the door closed behind them, I ran up the stairs to my bedroom. I cracked open a 99-cent notebook, flopped onto my bed and started writing. I wrote quickly before the details would evaporate from my memory.

It didn't matter that I wouldn't see him again because I would have the day recorded forever. Any time I wanted to spend time with Cruz, I could, just by reading my words.

This is how I write: I get an idea. From where? I don't know. Maybe from a muse or God, or maybe indigestion. I get a lot of indigestion.

Anyway, I get an idea, and I have to write it down. Have to. I'm kind of the crack addict of writers. I gotta. I needa. I hafta.

So, I get a pen—I love the XXL Bic pens, which are discontinued, but I can still find them at the 99-cent store—crack open one of my notebooks, and just write.

I mean, I don't know where the words come from, and I'm not even aware when I'm writing. I just zone out, and my hand flies across the paper, stringing words together in a reasonably good story.

I don't wake from my writing stupor until my fingers cramp too bad to hold the pen. Not only am I the crack addict of writers, I'm also the zombie of writers. I'm like The Walking Dead, but the Lying Down and Writing Dead.

So, I was crack/zombie writing, almost done with the last detail of my blissful time with beautiful Cruz—twenty pages front and back—when my mother threw open my door and stormed into my room.

She had taken off her bikini and had put on sweats and a hoodie. Her hair was tied back in a ponytail, and her eyes were big and bloodshot. She had the look on her face she got when she figured her life was crap, and I was most likely to blame.

She was too quick for me. She swiped my notebook out of my hands and held it high above her head.

"Are you kidding me?" she screeched. "You're up here playing around when I'm slaving away downstairs? Don't even think you're not going to help clean up."

I heard her voice as if it was coming from the other end of a long tunnel. My attention was on my notebook. As she spoke, she waved it around, making the precious pages flap. I knew I would have to be careful. Mom was volatile at best and at worst she knew how to hurt me.

"I'm sorry," I said, my voice a soft whisper. "I'll come down right now."

"I mean, you play, you pay, kid," she continued, screeching as loud as she could. "I noticed you had a pretty good time at the party and then you leave me to repair the damage."

She lowered the notebook and rolled it in her hands until it formed into a tight cylinder.

"You're right," I said.

Mom blinked, as if she was trying to focus on me. I noticed her attention had shifted to my body. My towel had slipped, revealing me in my bikini. Her face registered surprise and something that fueled her anger, and I quickly re-tied the towel around me.

"Damn right, I'm right," she said, enunciating each word slowly.

The room grew quiet. I had stopped breathing. We studied each other, me trying to read on her face what punishment she had planned for me, and her studying me to determine just how much she hated me at that moment.

I longed to be anywhere but there. There was nothing safe about my room, nothing safe about being anywhere where my mother could get at me. But I couldn't get away. I was sixteen, and I was invisible. My mother was the only person in my life.

Mom blinked and took a deep, deciding breath. Then, she opened my notebook and ripped a page in half. Then, another. Then, another. She grew calmer as she ripped. She ripped until my memories of Cruz laid on my bedroom floor, transformed into confetti.

"And mop the kitchen. It's a mess," she said as she left my room.

I dropped to the floor, gathered the bits of paper, and wished to be invisible once more.

Chapter 3

I'm nobody. Who are you?

--Emily Dickinson

The summer was over, and I was three-thousand-dollars richer. Not bad and almost worth babysitting the Maclaren triplets for three months.

After surviving taking care of the three, not-potty-trained toddlers--especially the time they got into the Costco supply of Hersheys and puked and pooped for six hours straight--I would have thought the first day back at school wouldn't have seemed so scary. But it was.

Poop and puke were nothing compared to high school students.

I opened the Danish butter cookies tin that I had hidden under my bed and counted the money that I had stashed there. Three-thousand-four-hundred-seventy five-dollars and twenty-three cents. That's how much closer I was to the Sorbonne in Paris.

I had enough for the plane but no way to survive once I was there, especially because I couldn't get a work visa and so couldn't work in France. I also had no idea how to apply to the Sorbonne or how much it cost. And after three years of high school

French, all I could say was: "Il y a de la neige sur le train," which means: "There's snow on the train."

"And bienvenue a Paris," I said to my empty bedroom. "Welcome to Paris. I know how to say that, too."

I was a wild-eyed optimist when it came to Paris. I had no idea how I would get there, but I was determined to do it. Get to Paris, study at the Sorbonne, and write all day at cafes on the Boulevard Saint-Germain-des-Prés. I knew deep in my heart that this was my ticket to happiness.

My ticket to me.

I threw my pocket Emily Dickinson book into my backpack, along with my binder, and zipped it closed. Emily had kept me company my whole life, ever since I learned to read. But she had been content to live her life in her room, and I had been counting down until I could escape my invisible life.

I slipped the backpack over my shoulders, my feet into flip-flops, and I ran downstairs. I poured coffee and water into the coffee maker and flipped the *on* switch. I placed two Pop Tarts into the toaster and got the milk out of the fridge.

Once it was done, I poured coffee into my mom's favorite mug and topped it with the milk. I was her alarm clock, because she wanted to be woken with a cup of coffee instead of top-forty tunes and a happy DJ. Nevertheless, it was hit or miss in the morning. I mean, her mood was all over the map before she got her caffeine.

I walked upstairs and opened her bedroom door. Inside

looked normal. All Disney princesses and Miss Havisham. Lace and pillow-topped everything. When in doubt, my mom liked to surround herself in whatever was appropriate for a five-year old girl.

The whole house looked like Goldilocks had thrown up all over it.

Mom's curtains were drawn, leaving only a crack of light peeking through. I put her coffee on the nightstand next to her bed, and I opened the curtains. The sun flooded in, illuminating every corner of her Laura Ashley ensemble.

But the sun had no effect on her. She was sound asleep.

"Good morning," I said, quietly, making my way to a safe distance away from her by the door. "7:15. Wakey. Wakey."

Mom stirred and turned onto her stomach. I had to get going, or I would be late for the first day of school.

"Okay, then," I said. "You're awake, right? The coffee is by your left arm. Wakey. Wakey."

I sighed. If I left without waking her, she would Godzilla my ass. It took her at least an hour to get ready for work. Her eyeliner and curling iron took up a good twenty minutes. If she was late, she would blame me, but I had to be careful. She only had limited patience for alarm clocks. I bit my lower lip. What to do?

"Ahem," I said.

"I heard you!" she yelled into her pillow. "What the hell! Just leave, already."

Phew. My work here was done. "Okay," I whispered.

"Leaving now."

I tiptoed out and ran down the stairs. Grabbing my Pop Tarts, I left the house, locking the front door behind me. *That went smoothly,* I thought. I had forgotten to remind her that it was the first day of school, but since I would be home way before she was, it didn't really matter.

My mother had defied all of my predictions and was still with The Boyfriend. It was probably her longest relationship. More often than not, she would sleep over at his house, or he would sleep at ours. Several times, I went in to wake her up in the morning but had to turn around in a hurry after taking in an eyeball-full of their canoodling.

Blech. Shudder.

I was right about Cruz. I never saw him again after the pool party. My mom and The Boyfriend never mentioned him—at least not in front of me—and I wondered if he was still in town or if he had given up on Mr. paella-and-wine and ran home to his mother.

After my mom had ripped apart my notebook, I opened another one and wrote all about Cruz. This time I wrote slowly. Every night when the house was dark and quiet, I would slip into bed and write by the light of a flashlight. I savored every word, every memory, dragging them out, detailing all my senses that he had awakened.

I filled two notebooks. Then, I kept writing. I wrote about the future. About possibilities.

Cruz possibilities.

I wasn't kidding myself. I knew there were no Cruz possibilities. I knew there were only Cruz impossibilities. I mean, I wasn't stupid. I wasn't certifiable.

But when you're invisible, living with a mother who would rather you'd disappear completely, writing about Cruz possibilities was a comfort. By the first day of school, I had written about Cruz and me starting a Bed & Breakfast, going on a romantic yet doomed mission to Mars, and starring in the Twilight reboot together. Among other stories.

Whenever I felt like I was living a Judy Blume novel or destined to be the new *Girl, Interrupted*, or that my dream to move to Paris was a ridiculous, impossible delusion, I would write about Cruz. With the movement of my Bic pen over my cheap paper, gone was the desperation, depression, and frankly, anger that stalked me morning, noon, and night.

A seething furious anger that I never allowed myself to feel.

I wondered if the Dalai Lama wrote about Cruz possibilities. I mean, he was always smiling.

It was a twelve-minute walk to school. I timed it to arrive right when the bell rang. My survival instinct prevented me from hanging around the quad before school started. Invisible sucked, but it was better than being a target. Getting there right when the bell rang meant that I could slip into class and into a seat in the back row without anybody taking notice of me.

I checked my schedule. I had humanities first period, which was usually my best class. Easy A. This year I had Mr.

Lawrence, who was a new teacher.

The room was packed. More budget cuts meant our class was bursting with forty-two seats. I took the one in the very back row next to the door just as the bell rang.

Mr. Lawrence was young and good looking. He wore jeans and a t-shirt announcing READ. He had round, wire-rimmed glasses that framed his big blue eyes. I could imagine he would be the object of a lot of high school girls' fantasies. His syllabus wouldn't help matters. *Pride & Prejudice, Love Story, Romeo and Juliet.* Mr. Lawrence was going to have to contend with a lot of lovesick seniors.

The students shifted in their seats, opening binders and notebooks, clicking their pens and twirling their pencils. The girls wore itty-bitty miniskirts, Daisy Dukes, or tighter than tight jeans. The boys sagged or didn't.

There was a sad lack of acne and a surprising amount of designer bags. Zac Posen might call it "pedestrian," but I called it "over my budget."

I was wearing jeans—normal ones, not tight—and a men's white undershirt. I had pulled my hair back into a ponytail, as usual.

I took out my binder and pencil and waited to take notes. Although I had already read everything on the reading list, I was still a fanatic about my grades. I didn't know what grades the

Sorbonne wanted, but I would be ready with A's. Come on Mr. Lawrence, I thought, bring it on. Make my day.

He started with attendance. About halfway through, he got to me. "Tess Parker," he called.

"Here," I said, quietly and raised my hand.

"You mean, *Mess* Parker," Jillian Glass sneered, causing a wave of snickering throughout the class.

I held my breath. "Mess" was one of the miseries I had lived with since second grade when I didn't know how to brush my hair.

I slumped down into my chair and waited for the snickering to stop. It wasn't a great way to start my senior year. The other students turned to look at me, as if the world had turned inside out, the back had become the front, and I had become the teacher.

I guessed they were trying to see if I really was a mess. I ran a self-conscious hand over my hair and fought a desire to close my eyes and run out of the room.

I would have wished for a miracle to happen, something to draw the attention away from me, something to erase "Mess Parker" from my fellow seniors' sadistic minds, but I didn't believe in miracles. In my experience, miracles were like unicorns. Like the Abominable Snowman. Like a good Adam Sandler movie.

Then, a unicorn pranced into the classroom.

I mean, a miracle happened.

The door burst open, and a wild creature marched through.

She wore a pink tutu and black leggings with boots, a t-shirt, and lots of bangle bracelets. Her head looked like it had exploded but instead of brain bits, blond curls shot out in frizzy, manic spikes. Like they were trying to escape or attack anyone who came too close to her.

She opened her large plastic purse and rummaged through it. Finally, she took out a scrap of paper.

"Is this humanities?" she asked, reading from the paper.

Then, her wallet fell out of her purse.

And a tampon.

All heads turned in unison from Mess Parker to the tampon on the floor. I was relieved but mortified for her. I couldn't imagine her recovering from the tampon incident.

It turned out that I didn't need to feel sorry for her. She didn't care in the least about revealing her Tampax Pearl Active Regular. She picked it up and looked at it like, "Oh, there it is" and tossed it back into her large purse.

"I hope it's humanities," she continued, not embarrassed at all. "This is my third classroom. I can't figure out the room numbers."

Mr. Lawrence stared at her with his mouth open, but no sound came out. The ticking of the clock grew louder. Then, the snickering resumed, but it was directed at her instead of me.

She joined in with the laughter, not realizing or not caring that they were laughing at her.

Finally, Mr. Lawrence remembered how to speak. "Take a seat, Miss--?"

"Dahlia. Dahlia Sherman."

She smiled ear to ear and took a seat, fighting against her tutu, which was bigger than the chair. She stuffed the tutu under the desk, her bangles clanging the whole time. She pulled a small glitter-covered notebook and a feather-topped pen out of her purse, crossed her legs, and sat back like she was ready to take on the world and she was on a cruise or somewhere else equally fabulous.

"Phew," she said to me. "What a morning. I never thought I would find the class."

Oh, yeah. Did I mention that she sat next to me?

"Uh," I said.

"I'm Dahlia," she said, extending her hand. I shook it. "New, of course. You probably already guessed that." She rolled her eyes.

Mr. Lawrence was handing out textbooks and giving instructions on how to write our names in the books.

"Yay," she announced, showing me her book. "No penis drawings in mine. Usually I get the one packed with penises."

I showed her mine. There was a drawing of a penis every

ten pages or so.

"Circumcised," Dahlia said, nodding. "Nice."

Weirdly, Dahlia and I had all the same classes until lunch. For the first time since I was eight, school flew by. I was almost happy to be there. I was having fun. Dahlia was crazy weird. She giggled in math class, pirouetted in biology, and couldn't stop talking to me.

To me.

She talked about global warming, ballet, Adam Levine, and butter. She talked about everything and anything and all the stuff in between. And she was happy, like she had the happy gene and not even high school could bring her down.

She was the coolest person I had ever met.

The lunch bell rang, and Dahlia followed me to the cafeteria. I typed in my pin number for free lunch. We both got the chicken sandwich and chocolate milk.

"This is so much better than my last school in Virginia," she said, taking a seat across from me. "That was more like Alcatraz than a high school."

"Virginia?"

"My dad's in the military," she explained. "We move around all the time. Virginia, New York, San Francisco, Paris—"

My ears perked up. "Paris? You've been to Paris?"

"Eighteen months. Have you been there?"

"I haven't been anywhere."

Dahlia shrugged and smiled ear to ear. "I've been enough places for both of us."

Lunch was over before I knew it. We said goodbye because Dahlia had drama and cheerleading, while I had computers and study hall.

The rest of the day I thought about having a friend who had been to Paris, about having a friend at all. Period.

That's why I spent the rest of the day at school in a great mood. And why I went home in a great mood. And why I stayed in a great mood right up until I walked through the front door and was surprised by my mother, who was home from work in the middle of the day. She had packed two large suitcases and was wheeling them through the entry on her way out.

Leaving me.

Chapter 4

Anger as soon as fed is dead—'Tis starving that makes it fat.

--Emily Dickinson

My mother was in a great mood, too. Much better mood than simply finding a new friend, she was resplendent with the joy that comes with true, new beginnings.

I knew that look. It was the look I had imagined on my face each time I fantasized about going to Paris. Like a new bride or a new mother or the first day of a really great job, my mom was glowing with the anticipation that her life was taking a right turn.

"What's going on?" I asked her. "Are you going somewhere?"

"There you are. I was going to leave you a note," she said, taking a look at herself in the hallway mirror. "I'm getting picked up any minute now."

"Where are you going?"

"We're going to Mexico!" she announced, hopping in her high heels, giddy with excitement.

"Out of the country?" I asked. "We? You mean with your boyfriend?"

"Who else?" she said and adjusted her boobs in her push-up bra. Then, she looked and me and scowled, forming lines between her eyes. "No attitude from you. It's just for a few months."

"A few months!"

A few months? She was just going to pick up and leave me for a few months?

A car horn blared outside, and my mom wheeled her suitcases outside, nudging me out of her path. "Water the plants," she said over her shoulder.

I stood on the front porch with my mouth wide open. I was startled, shocked, freaking out.

A few months?

The Boyfriend hopped out of the car and put Mom's suitcases in the trunk of his BMW. He opened the passenger door for her, and she slid inside and took a seat.

"Don't give me that face," she called to me through the open window, as The Boyfriend started up the car. "It's not like you'll be on the streets. Besides, you won't be alone. We're sending Cruz to watch you."

And then she was gone. Off to Mexico for a few months.

I watched The Boyfriend's car race down the street, away from me. I stood and stared until it was long gone and only the quiet street remained with its rows of small track homes and palm trees.

"We don't have any plants. How can I water plants we don't have?" I finally said, although my mother couldn't hear me because she was miles away inside a BMW, probably listening to 80s music, and on her way to the border.

Aloneness descended on me, wrapping around my body and squeezing tight until I couldn't breathe. For that moment there, standing on the front porch—alone, alone, alone—there was nobody else in the world. At least, there was nobody else in the world who cared about my existence or even knew about my existence.

It was like I had a force field around me and nobody would ever break through. Alone. I had out-Emily Dickinsoned Emily Dickinson.

Like a person falling off a cliff and seeing his life pass before his eyes, I thought of every bad thing that could happen to a sixteen-year old girl, alone without any support or supervision for a few months.

There were serial killers, hit-and-run drivers, appendicitis emergencies, and starvation. There were house fires and home invasions and tooth abscesses. Just to name a few.

It wasn't like my mother was all that supportive when she was around. For all intents and purposes, I took care of myself. Besides, she had left me before—many times—but not for more than a week, and she had warned me beforehand.

And she paid the rent.

Who was going to pay the rent?

Did she leave money for the rent?

Oh my God.

I was hit by a bolt of lightning. Not the kind of bolt that leaves you dead near the ninth hole at the golf course. This bolt of lightning was the "ah-ha" kind of bolt, the kind that hits you and tells you that you are so S.O.L. that you might as well kiss your future goodbye because you are screwed.

Screwed.

Screwed and poor and destined to be thrown into the street.

I ran inside the house without bothering to close the door behind me. I threw my backpack off and took the stairs two at a time. I was still running when I got to my bedroom, hurled myself onto the floor and crawled under my bed.

I grabbed my Danish Butter Cookies tin and opened it.

I gasped, taking in air but forgetting to breathe.

Empty. Nothing. Not a dollar. Not a cent. Not even a cookie crumb.

"No. No. No. No," I moaned.

I looked again, as if I had missed seeing a big wad of cash in the metal container the first time around.

Nope. Empty.

Gone was my Maclaren poop and puke money. Gone was my ticket to Paris money. And now that I was alone, gone was my survival money.

My head dropped to the floor and nestled in the deep shag carpeting. I lay like that, face down, under my bed for I don't know how long.

There was no reason to move. I was safe under my bed. There were no serial killers under there. Ditto bill collectors. If I could just stay under my bed, I reasoned, I would be okay.

Then, my stomach rumbled, which reminded me that I didn't have money to eat, which reminded me that I needed to eat—I had a very big appetite, usually—every day, in fact several times a day, which made me start to cry. Weep, actually.

I was weeping pretty good with a whole snot thing happening and was about to erupt in a "why me?" whiny song when I was interrupted.

"Hello?" a man's voice called from downstairs.

I froze.

"Hello!"

It was a serial killer voice. A rapist, burglar, home invader, Hannibal Lecter voice. I had left the front door open, and now I was going to die a horrible death.

I turned on my side and wiped the snot off my face with

the hem of my t-shirt. What to do? My cell phone was in my backpack downstairs. So no 911, and I couldn't protect myself. I didn't have a weapon, not even a baseball bat because I had never been into sports.

Why wasn't I sporty? If I had been sporty, I wouldn't be about to be murdered by the star of *Saw III*.

"Hello?" he called again. "Tess? It's me, Cruz."

"Oh, my God, I've gone delusional in my last moments of life," I said to my empty room. "Help. Help. I'm hearing things. I've gone crazy. I'm Brittany Spears shaving her head."

I heard the serial killer climb the stairs in a hurry. A second later, he was tapping my leg, which was sticking out from under the bed.

"Tess? It's me. Cruz. You under there?" He tapped again, and I stuck my fingers in my ears.

"Don't hurt me," I squeaked.

His hands wrapped around my ankles, and he pulled. I glided over the carpet out from under the bed in one swift movement. Cruz leaned over me, one of his eyebrows raised up to his hairline, as if he were questioning my sanity, and he probably was.

He was beautiful. More handsome than I remembered. I was amazed at how my mind could conjure up an exact replica of Cruz right before I was going to be killed. With the power of my brain, I had transformed a serial killer into a gorgeous, perfect boy. Talk about wishful thinking. I was a master.

"Tess, it's me," he said. I noticed that his serial killer voice was gone and his soft, deep, comforting voice was back. I blinked and wiped my eyes.

"Cruz?" I asked.

"What were you doing under there?"

"I thought she was joking," I said. "I thought she was teasing me about you coming."

He gently lifted a strand of my hair that had fallen over my face, and tucked it behind my ear. "Your mom?" he asked.

"She left with your dad."

"I know. He called me this morning."

"She said they would be gone for months."

He nodded and sat cross-legged next to me. "He got a job in Puerta Vallarta."

"A job?"

"He's very excited about it."

I sat up. "So he left you alone in the condo?" I asked him.

"No, he gave up the condo," Cruz said. "Besides, he kicked me out two weeks ago."

"Why?"

Cruz shrugged. "Why. Good question. But I'm here now."

He stood and helped me up.

"Did he leave you money?" I asked.

"No."

"Oh my God," I breathed. I kept hearing *Doomed! Doomed!* over and over in my head.

"Let's go downstairs and take stock of our situation," he said, wisely. I studied his face. Serious but kind. And something else, concerned for me.

I nodded. For the first time since my mother left, I felt safe and secure. In addition to his beauty, there was a calm strength about him.

I followed Cruz downstairs. His back was as good as his front. He had wide shoulders and narrow hips, and he turned around twice to make sure I was following him. Of course, I was following him. I would have followed him anywhere.

Chapter 5

Where thou art, that is home.

--Emily Dickinson

We weren't alone. There were two other people in the house. A guy and a girl, both older than me. Both way more good-looking and well dressed.

"Everything alright?" The guy asked Cruz. He was tall and slim, with a perfect face and body, like he had been constructed by GQ Magazine. He wore a tight black suit and shiny shoes, and I noticed his fingernails were manicured. Buffed.

"Yeah," Cruz said. "Fine. Eric, Dana, this is Tess."

They looked me up and down. Dana took stock of me quickly and looked away, probably feeling that I wasn't worth her time. She was gorgeous, heavily made up, wispy thin with skyscraper high heels.

It was like they were vampires. You know, the Twilight kind. Perfect, beautiful, young. I wanted them to bite me and make me beautiful, too, but no such luck. They didn't seem to have a craving for Emily Dickinson girl.

"Hi, Tess," Eric said, shaking my hand. "I guess we'll go, now. Dana has a shoot. I can take you to school tomorrow, if you want, Cruz."

"Awesome," Cruz said.

And then they were gone, leaving a trail of swagger behind them. They didn't look like high school kids. They were way too cool for that. More like they had just hopped off a yacht at the Cannes Film Festival.

Cruz closed the door behind his gorgeous friends. I noticed a suitcase in the corner, which I assumed belonged to him. He ignored it and walked with me into the kitchen.

"Maybe she left you survival money or a note with instructions," he said.

We searched for about an hour. We scoured every drawer, ever table. Besides a dirty cup and bowl in the sink, my mother had left me nothing. I wasn't surprised. I mean, if she cleaned out my cookie tin, I didn't think she was going to leave me any presents.

No presents. No money. No survival.

I didn't need much, but I really liked showers. And my bed. I had slept in my bed every night since I could remember. I had gotten attached.

Now I was headed to Skid Row, and I didn't think I could bring my bed or my shower with me. With my fate as a future bag lady sealed, I lost my ability to swallow. I started to hyperventilate.

"Whoa," Cruz said. "You're turning blue. Breathe. Don't panic. All is not lost. Why don't you call her? Ask survival questions."

I got my cell phone and dialed her number. On the second ring, her familiar Taylor Swift's "Shake It Off" ringtone went off on the couch. My mother had left her cell phone behind.

"What the—" I picked it up and turned it off.

"Her phone plan probably doesn't cover Mexico," Cruz explained. "My dad warned me that I couldn't call him. That's why she left it."

It was like I was Robinson Crusoe but in the suburbs and with homework. Like Tom Hanks on a raft. I was shipwrecked in my house.

"May I panic, now?"

Cruz emptied his pockets onto the kitchen counter. "I've got fourteen dollars and change. How much do you have?"

I couldn't bring myself to tell him about the cookie tin, about how my mother had not only stolen my money but had stolen my dreams. I couldn't even say it out loud.

"I'm broke," I said. "The Maclaren triplets are in daycare, but I might be able to pick up some babysitting hours on the weekend."

"I've got an interview for a job at Neiman Marcus," Cruz said. "And hopefully I'll get some modeling gigs. I'm hungry. Let's see what we can scrounge up."

We figured we had enough food to last until the end of the week. I could eat two meals a day at school during the week, and Cruz, it turned out, was on a diet because he was becoming a model.

Meanwhile, I made macaroni and cheese, and he put together two ham sandwiches. We moved around the kitchen together without saying a word. My brain swirled with thoughts of my new reality, about whether I would be able to stay in school, keep my grades up, and manage to make it to Paris.

Nope. It was like pooping in space. I couldn't figure out a way to do it.

Cruz opened the refrigerator, and I took out the milk. He put slices of bread on the counter, and I handed him the ham. He cut the sandwiches into four pieces, just like I liked it. We worked with each other naturally, as if we had been preparing meals together all our lives. Like we belonged together.

It was a lifesaver, having him there. You know, in a Twilight Zone what-is-a-beautiful-boy-doing-in-my-house kind of way. I don't know what I would have done if he hadn't shown up. He was my crutch, a hero figure, my knight with fourteen dollars and an interview at Neiman Marcus.

We took the food and migrated outside to the table next to the pool, where we had sat a month before and talked about nice things instead of the possibility of becoming homeless. It turned out that Cruz had already been homeless for the past two weeks.

"Friends have been letting me sleep on their couches," he explained, as we ate. "It's just until I get a job. I know the manager at the men's cologne counter at Neiman's. She said she can hook me up. It's minimum wage plus commission."

"That's great," I said. "Are you sure you can do that with school?"

Cruz ran his fingers through his hair and grinned, forming two dimples on his cheeks. "I kind of quit school."

"But your friend Eric said he was taking you tomorrow."

"Oh, well. You see—" He grinned again, and I realized he grinned when he was embarrassed. "I'm going because there's this thing. It's stupid. You don't want to hear about it."

"Oh, sure," I said. "I understand if you don't want to tell me."

I was hurt that he didn't want to share with me, but I wasn't surprised. After all, I was still surprised that he was speaking to me. Sharing was another thing altogether. A few notches up. Like surf 'n' turf instead of a Big Mac value meal.

Already, he had given me more attention and consideration than I had ever received from another person. But there was a line he wouldn't cross. He didn't want me to get too close. I wasn't surprised, but I was disappointed.

Cruz was like potato chips. I couldn't be satisfied. One taste and I wanted the whole bag.

But I was wrong about the line he wouldn't cross, wrong about him not wanting to share himself with me. Cruz would always be generous. He would give and give and never hold back where I was concerned.

In fact, later, he would give me too much. He would love me and cherish me, and out of that love would come pain and more. But sitting there by the pool the day my mother abandoned me, I didn't understand the other side of love. Why would I? I had no experience with that particular emotion.

"Don't forget I warned you that it was stupid," Cruz said, grinning. "I'm sort of in a play."

"A play?"

"Promise you won't laugh."

I nodded. "Cross my heart."

Cruz took a deep breath. "Okay. It's a musical. West Side Story. I'm Chino. It's not a big part, which is a good thing because I can't sing or dance or act. Are you smiling or laughing?"

"Smiling!" I said. "I think it's great."

"Yeah. So, I'm holding on to do the part Friday night. Otherwise, I've quit school. I've been busy working on getting a portfolio together for modeling. Eric has been helping me."

I nodded. I was unclear about Eric's role in Cruz's life, but I didn't feel like I could ask him. Besides, I had other things to think about.

"Maybe I should quit school, too," I said. "Get a job."

I swallowed back tears. My hopes and dreams of going to

the Sorbonne were being snatched away, replaced with being a high school dropout and trying to find a job to keep me out of the homeless shelter.

"Nah," Cruz said. "You're a minor. If you drop out, they'll come looking for you. You'll wind up in foster care. I think you need to act as normal as possible. Go to school, get some babysitting hours. We'll work this out."

Tears rolled down my cheeks. I was so grateful to him for letting me stay in school, for telling me I would be okay.

You know, for lying to me.

"We'll throw away all the bills unless they have 'shut off notice' written on the envelope," he explained. "That'll give us time. Eric said I'll be able to get modeling gigs pretty quickly."

"Okay," I breathed.

Cruz wiped a tear off my cheek with his thumb. "Pretty girls shouldn't cry," he said.

Cruz took the third bedroom, which was more or less a tiny storage room with a single bed. We left my mother's room empty. We spent the evening sitting on the couch, watching *Big Bang Theory* reruns, while I did my homework.

I guess Cruz's calm and positive attitude didn't help me as much as I thought because I woke up screaming at two in the morning. I had been having a nightmare that my mother was smothering me with her pillow. As she tried to kill me, she shouted, "Go away! Go away!"

I gasped and sputtered and flailed my arms, but I couldn't get her off of me. Just as I thought I would die, Cruz woke me up.

"It's just a dream," he said in his soft, deep voice. I opened my eyes to see him leaning over me. He wore boxers with no shirt. It occurred to me that I might still be dreaming.

"You were dreaming," he continued. "Bad dream."

"My mother was trying to kill me," I croaked.

"Yeah, I figured," he said. "Is it okay if I stay with you until you get back to sleep?"

"Aren't you tired?"

"Move over."

I scooched over, and he lay down next to me, covering us both with the blanket. He was warm, and he smelled clean like a forest after a rain.

"I hate nightmares," he said.

"Me too. Normally I don't remember my dreams."

"I do. It's like a movie theater in there," he said, pointing at his head.

"This one was so real."

"Dream about money this time, Tess. Or steak. I'd love a steak."

"I'll do my best," I said.

"Sleep, now. You have an early morning."

"Okay," I said, but I knew I would never be able to fall asleep with Cruz in bed with me. He was half-naked, only inches away from my body. He was giving off an electrical current that hit me in my belly and made me dizzy, even while lying down. It would be impossible to relax enough to sleep, I reasoned. I would be awake the rest of the night, focused on the position of his body compared to mine, focused on the possibility that my hand would travel and rest on his. Focused on the possibility that he might want to hold me, to touch me. No, I would never be able to sleep like that.

But I was wrong. Lying there next to Cruz, I was asleep within seconds. I slept the sleep of a person who was cared for. Soundly.

Chapter 6

Truth is so rare that it is delightful to tell it.

--Emily Dickinson

So, now I was living with a boy.

Let me repeat that: I was living with a boy.

I was living with a boy who wasn't my brother or cousin, and he was gorgeous and was nice to me. Yes, I did pinch myself to see if I was dreaming. I was black and blue from all the pinching.

I had never lived with any kind of boy. No brothers. No cousins. So, I didn't have much to compare. But now, by definition, I was living the end of a romance novel. I was living with Mr. Darcy, Edward Cullen, and Romeo, himself. By all accounts, I was the luckiest girl in the world.

However.

However, we weren't in a romance.

No kissing. No handholding.

In fact, Cruz went out every night without me. Eric, Dana, or other perfectly beautiful people would pick him up at the house, they would finalize his outfit and man-beautify him some more with hair products and facial moisturizer, and off they would go into the night. He wouldn't come home until long after I was asleep.

It was a lot like living with my mother, except that Cruz was nice, and I didn't have to wake him up in the morning. I did have to clean up after him, though. He seemed to belong to a religion that didn't believe in hanging up wet towels.

How fun to play house, you might think. Cooking with Cruz, cleaning up after Cruz, sleeping across the hall from Cruz. But we were playing house only in as much as *The Outsiders* were playing house.

I mean, we watched our food supply dwindle, and we threw away the bills, unopened. We sat on the couch watching TV every afternoon, holding our breath, in fear that Child Protective Services would find out that I was abandoned and put me in Foster care and throw Cruz out onto the street.

Fun times.

Every time the home phone rang, I would leap for it, but it was never my mother, never The Boyfriend. If it weren't for the frilly, lacy stuff around the house, I would have thought my mother had never existed. She had disappeared in a puff of BMW exhaust and not a word from her since.

It was absolutely crucial that we kept our predicament top secret. Since my only friend was Dahlia, that wasn't too hard. And Cruz's friends had no interest in me. Obviously, I wasn't one of the beautiful people and didn't rate.

I had no problem keeping the giant secret. I didn't need to tell anyone, because I wrote every last detail down in my notebooks. I could write pages on Cruz sneezing, alone. Ditto for the way he walked, how he ate. I was fascinated by everything he did, and I was desperate to figure out what he was thinking.

Sometimes when I was with him, I would have to bite my lip not to ask him, "What are you thinking about?" I had read enough books to know that boys hate when girls ask them what they're thinking. But I wanted to know his innermost thoughts. I wanted to know every time a neuron fired up in his brain. If I had been a zombie, I would have eaten his brain first.

For sure.

Cruz was a fathomless, inscrutable mystery, as far as I was concerned. He didn't seem all that worried about being a high school dropout, without any family and no way to make a living. He seemed happy.

Weird, right?

But there were moments, infinitesimal, tiny moments where he would catch my eye, and I would see something travel over his face. What was it? Worry? Anxiety? I had no clue.

"What are your plans for the weekend?" Dahlia asked me that Friday morning in humanities class. It was the end of the first week of school. Day four of living with Cruz. Despite her quirkiness, Dahlia had become extremely popular in school.

Cheerleader, star of the school play, it didn't matter that Dahlia wore outlandish clothes and spoke whatever was on her mind. She had been immediately thrust into the cool crowd.

That's why it was so strange that she still talked to me, still sat with me at lunch. She was determined to be my friend, and I soaked up every moment in her light. Dahlia was all light and no shadow. Fresh.

"Uh, actually I'm going to a play a friend is in," I told her. "I mean, after I babysit."

Mrs. Maclaren promised to give me ten hours of babysitting a week. Two hours, five days a week in the evening. She was actually relieved when I asked her for work during the school year. With triplets, she explained, she needed all the help she could get.

Ten hours a week would keep me in food and notebooks, but God help me if I needed new panties or the city was going to shut off our water. I put out fliers for more babysitting work. I was hoping for steady babysitting on the weekends. Ten more hours would allow me to breathe easier.

I couldn't get a regular job, like at McDonald's, because I needed a work permit, and I needed a parent's permission for that. So, I had to work for cash only.

"A play? How exciting!" Dahlia exclaimed, drawing stares from the other students. "What play?"

"West Side Story," I said. "He's Chino."

"He?" Dahlia asked me, grinning madly, as if I had told her I was having an affair with Liam Hemsworth. "Your boyfriend?"

"Yes," was on the tip of my tongue. I wanted to lie to her, play out all my fantasies about Cruz. *Yes, he's my boyfriend. We're passionately in love, and he wants to marry me,* I wanted to say. But Dahlia was my best friend, my only friend, and I couldn't lie to her about Cruz. I could lie about my mother, but not about Cruz.

"Nah, I don't have a boyfriend. He's just someone I know," I said.

"Yeah, right," she said, winking at me. "Tess and Chino sitting in tree," she sang.

I giggled. It was the first time someone thought I could have a boyfriend, and it made me feel great.

"K-I-S-S-I-N-G," she sang even louder.

Everyone was staring now. For the first time in my life, I didn't care, because it was about Cruz. With him in my life, I felt stronger, more like a whole person.

"I'd go with you," Dahlia told me as we walked to our next class. "But I have this stupid cheerleading thing. There's always a party, you know. Hey, if you're not busy with Chino next week, can you go with me? I would have a lot more fun with you there."

A cheerleading party.

Me.

It was like she was asking me to go with her to an island of cannibals while I wore a meat suit. Who was I kidding? A cheerleading party was exactly like an island of cannibals, and for sure if I were there, they would treat me like I was wearing a meat suit. I would be eaten alive.

"I don't know," I said. "I'll have to check my schedule."

I didn't actually have a schedule. Since I never went anywhere, there wasn't much need for calendars in my life. But I didn't want Dahlia to know that cheerleaders terrified me, and I didn't want her to realize that I was invisible girl at school and that it was total popular-girl suicide to hang out with me.

"No worries," she said. "And we can get chili cheese fries, after. Did I tell you I got a car? A Toyota Corolla. Not the coolest car in the lot, but my dad promised to paint it purple."

I was covered in baby upchuck. I was also twenty-five dollars richer, so I couldn't complain too much about the puke. But I needed to change fast out of my barf babysitting clothes in order to catch the bus to go to Cruz's school or I would miss his play. What to wear to a perfect boy's play? I didn't exactly have an I-love-a-perfect-boy wardrobe. I took a quick shower (picking up Cruz's wet towels, first), sprayed on some perfume, pulled my hair back in a ponytail and threw on jeans and a turtleneck, even though it was ninety degrees out. I thought about makeup. I did have lip gloss and mascara, but I had only put them on twice before.

I decided not to brave the mascara wand, but I swiped on the gloss, grabbed my bus pass, and locked the door behind me.

I caught the bus just as it reached my corner, but it took

longer to get to Cruz's school than I had anticipated. By the time I arrived, the play had already started, and I had to stand in the back of the auditorium.

Cruz was right. He couldn't sing or dance or act, but he was the most beautiful boy on stage. There was no way Maria would pick Tony over Chino, I thought. Any girl would pick Chino. Any blind girl would pick Chino.

It was that obvious.

Sure, Tony could act and sing and he looked a lot like Justin Timberlake, but Chino was Cruz. Cruz didn't even need to say or sing a word. Just standing on stage, he had an electrical magnetism that drew everyone's attention. He was simply a star.

The play ended in standing ovations and a roar of applause. I moved forward toward the stage with the crowd. It was bedlam with aggressive parents and their cell phone cameras, intent on taking as many pictures of their costume-wearing children as possible.

I wanted to congratulate Cruz, but I couldn't get near him. He was surrounded by kids and parents trying to get close to him, to touch him, and tell him how wonderful he was. He made the rounds, shaking hands and hugging. He was the most popular member of the cast, most likely the most popular student at the school even though he had only been there about a month.

I stepped closer, and I got an elbow in the side from a girl with a Chanel bag, fake eyelashes, and shorts so short that I could see butt cheeks.

"Excuse me," she said like she didn't want me to excuse her

at all. "Take a number, Nanook of the North. As if."

She pushed ahead, managing to get close enough to Cruz to wrap her leg around his and hug him for all he was worth. She whispered something in his ear, and he nodded and grinned, embarrassed.

It was a good time to turn around and catch the next bus back home. Why was I even there? I wasn't part of Cruz's crowd. Sure, he lived with me and ate mac and cheese with me, but I was nowhere close to being in his social circle.

He was Bora Bora, and I was Siberia. He was Jay Z, and I was Urkel. His cool factor was off the charts, and my cool factor was minus three.

I turned around and took a step towards the door, when I caught another elbow. I snapped my head around, ready for a fight.

"Hey, where are you going? Was I that bad?" Cruz put his hand on the small of my back and urged me towards the door.

"What? No!" I tried to say, but with his hand on me like that, I'm pretty sure it came out: "Gurgle. Gurgle. Sputter. Gack."

"Thanks for coming," he said. "I don't want to go to this thing alone. You can be my good luck charm."

"Where?" He held the door open for me, and I stepped through it.

"Neiman Marcus. My interview. If it goes well, I'll spring for a steak."

"Steak," I said. "Yeah, right."

"A hamburger on the dollar menu, then," he said.

We took the bus to Fashion Valley mall. Cruz seemed to have forgotten that he had just been in a play and got a standing ovation. He seemed to forget, too, that he was officially a high school dropout. One minute he was the center of attention and the next minute he was alone on a bus with me.

"Are you nervous about your interview?" I asked him.

He shrugged his shoulders. "I hope I get it," he said. "But I was told it's kind of a sure thing. It's just until, you know, I become a model."

"I think you'll be a great model," I said.

"You do?"

"Yes." Duh. He was a walking magazine ad. Didn't he realize that?

I had never been to Neiman Marcus before. There was no reason to. I couldn't afford anything in the store. Also, I couldn't fit in anything in the store.

Neiman Marcus was a department store for very, very rich, skinny people. Their customer base was Miley Cyrus or nothing.

"Holy cow," I said. I was looking straight up at the crystal chandeliers. My mouth had dropped open, and I had stopped blinking. "Talk about hoity-toity. This place is Versailles."

"What's Versailles?" Cruz asked. "Never mind. How do I look?"

He wore tight jeans, shiny shoes, and a button-down shirt. He was breathtaking, of course.

"Perfect," I said.

"Do I fit in? Would you buy men's cologne from me?"

I would have bought fermented cheese from him. I would have bought a barbed-wire bra from him. He was going to get really rich from commissions.

"I think so," I said.

He looked over at the men's cologne department. "I see her," he told me. "Stay around here. I'll come back after the interview, and we'll go for our hamburger."

I watched him head towards the cologne, and I milled about, looking at price tags. Holy smokes, who could imagine skinny jeans could cost twelve-hundred dollars? Were they made of diamonds?

"May I help you?" Elvira the vampire lady, dressed all in black from her head to her toes was giving me the stink eye. Her "may I help you" was really "what the hell are you doing here?"

"Just browsing," I said.

She arched her eyebrow and sniffed.

"Perhaps I can help with your browsing. Perhaps I could suggest JCPenny. It's at the other end of the mall."

Usually—I mean for my entire life—her attitude would make me say, "I'm sorry" and run out of the store with my tail between my legs. But like *Alien,* something had wormed its way into me and had started to transform me. I don't know if it was the fact that I had come there with a gorgeous boy who was going to get a hamburger with me after, or if it was the fact that I had a new friend, who was crazy and fun and popular, too.

Whatever the cause, I didn't run away from Elvira, the vampire saleslady. Instead, I took the diamond skinny jeans off the rack and handed them to her.

"I think I'll try this on," I said with a slight English accent to make me sound Neiman Marcus snobby. "Start a dressing room for me, will you?"

Our eyes locked, like we were having a staring match. I had never had a staring match before, but I was sure I wouldn't blink. There was no way I was going to let Elvira win. Obviously, I wasn't going to buy the jeans. Even if I sold our house—if we owned it and didn't rent it—I couldn't have afforded the jeans. Besides that, I couldn't fit my arm into it, let alone a leg.

But I wasn't going to let Elvira know that. So I didn't blink. I didn't back down.

After what seemed like hours, she took the jeans from me. "Fine. I'll set that right up," she said, smiling. She turned on her high heel and walked away.

I broke out in a huge sweat, and I wiped my forehead with

my sleeve. I thought I had better leave well enough alone and snuck out of Elvira's department to make my way to the men's cologne department. I wasn't going to bother Cruz during his interview, but I didn't think a little spying would be so bad. And I wanted to get as far away from Elvira as possible.

I found Cruz pretty quickly. He stood at the counter, speaking to an older lady, who stood on the other side of the counter, dressed all in black with long blond hair and a lot of makeup. Her face didn't move when she talked, and she was the one doing all the talking.

Her lips were colored a deep red. Every few seconds, she would touch Cruz, as if she was punctuating her sentences. She touched his hand, then his arm, then his shoulder, and finally, she caressed his cheek with a long, pointy fingernail. It was more than flirting. It was possession.

It was: You get naked with me, and I'll give you a job. It was wrong and unfair.

I shivered.

Suddenly, everything was clear. Suddenly, I understood what was really going on. I didn't need to read Cruz's mind. He didn't have to tell me a thing. I knew how much the job meant to him, how much he felt he needed it.

I also knew he could spend months sleeping on friends' couches. That way, he wouldn't have to worry about paying for electricity, water, or anything. But that wouldn't help *me*. I would need help, need someone to help take care of me, and so, here he was, standing stock still, listening intently to the old woman whose face didn't move.

And he was nodding. He was telling her, yes.

I wanted to cry. I wanted to shout out to him to stop. But I didn't. Something told me deep inside that I would humiliate him if I let him know that I knew what was happening. I didn't want to embarrass him, especially now that I knew just how good he was.

I hovered over the belts, pretending to be fascinated by buckles, while I spied on Cruz out of the corner of my eye. The interview only took a few minutes, and then Cruz walked over to me.

"I'm going to have to take a rain check on our hamburger," he said, studying the belts with more than normal curiosity. In fact, he wouldn't look me in the eye.

"Everything okay?"

"Yeah, it's just that the interview is going to continue—you know—when she's done working."

"Oh," I said, checking out the belts, again. "No problem. I'll catch a bus back."

We didn't say goodbye. We didn't look at each other. There was an undercurrent of understanding between us, but we didn't speak it out loud.

Going home on the bus at night alone was a dicey prospect. I sat up close to the bus driver, but that didn't stop a guy in a knit cap and face tattoos from telling me I was pretty and that he liked my boobs.

I longed for a car of my own so I wouldn't have to risk getting raped, kidnapped, or murdered on a bus at night. I longed for Mace, the tattoo guy, to leave me alone. I longed for Cruz to keep me company.

I didn't long for a hamburger, though. I had lost my appetite.

I lay wide-awake in bed until two in the morning when I heard the front door finally open. I heard Cruz's soft footsteps as he climbed the stairs and went directly into the bathroom and turned on the shower.

I waited in the dark of my bedroom for what seemed like forever. He was taking the world's longest shower. Finally, the water was turned off, and then I heard it: a soft whimpering like a puppy or a wounded child.

I got out of bed and knocked on the bathroom door.

"Cruz, are you okay?" I asked.

No answer. The whimpering stopped, though.

"I'm coming in," I announced through the door. "So, don't be naked."

I slowly turned the doorknob and opened the door. Inside,

the bathroom was filled with steam. After it cleared slightly, I could make out Cruz's form, sitting on the floor in the corner against the bathtub, wrapped in a towel, his head in his hands.

I sat on the floor next to him and pulled his head down to rest on my shoulder. I touched his arm, just a slight caress to calm him and make him feel better.

"I got the job," he said. "Twenty-five hours a week."

"That's great," I said.

He was quiet a long time, seemingly content to sit like that, his head on my shoulder, my hand on his arm.

"I had to go to her place." He spoke so quietly, I wasn't sure that he had actually spoken or if I had imagined it. But now I understood him, that he was as scared as I was, that the world was terrifying and hard, even for a perfectly beautiful boy who would probably become a famous model.

And I understood even more than that about Cruz. But it wasn't something I could vocalize or even write down.

"Thank you," I said. "Thank you for taking care of me."

Chapter 7

Behavior is what a man does, not what he thinks, feels, or believes.

--Emily Dickinson

"What is this?" Dahlia asked me in the cafeteria line.

"There was a debate about it last year," I said.

She lifted her plate to eye-level and studied Hoover High's attempt at providing healthy lunches for its students.

"A real debate?" Dahlia asked.

I nodded. "Most of the students think it's squirrel, but I heard the lunch ladies talking. It's a veggie burger. It's the alfalfa sprouts that make it look like that."

"I've never seen alfalfa sprouts do this."

"I think it's the way they fry them," I said.

"Do you think it's safe?"

"No. Joey Franklin swears he got diverticulitis from eating one. I'm doing double chips today." On veggie burger day, I usually went with a bag of Cheetos and backed it up with a bag of Baked Lays, just to stay on the healthy side.

Actually, I wasn't afraid of the veggie burger. I had lived off school food for about thirteen years and had successfully digested far scarier "food" than Hoover High's veggie burger.

I could recall a fish sandwich in fourth grade that took down the entire school with grade A food poisoning, but I came out of it with nary a burp.

I had a survivalist, industrial-strength stomach.

I was the Liam Neeson of digestive juices.

Dahlia gave her plate back to the lunch lady. "Wise," she said and picked up two bags of Chex Mix and put it on her tray. She threw a package of Oreos onto mine. "But we should stay away from soda since we're eating junk food for lunch."

"How about chocolate milk, then?" I suggested.

"Perfect."

Dahlia and I had fallen into a nice routine in the month we had known each other. Every day we would sit next to each other in our morning classes. I would help her in humanities, and she would help me in math. Then we would eat together, even though the "in" crowd tried to get Dahlia over to their table several times.

The first time Jillian Glass, the head of the cheerleading squad, came over to our table to try and recruit her, Dahlia turned it around. "Why don't you sit with *us*?" she asked the mean girl. "There's plenty of room."

Asking someone to defect from the popular table was like

asking Abraham Lincoln to change sides in the Civil War.

Not happening.

So not done.

Jillian scowled, mumbled "What ev'," and stormed away, tossing her long hair.

Dahlia didn't seem to notice. She was constantly happy, as if she was in a happiness bubble. A tough, The Rock kind of strong bubble that couldn't be popped.

Nothing and nobody got her down. She was happy to cheer with the cheerleaders, emote with the drama geeks, trade eyeliners with the socs, and eat lunch with the invisible girl.

She was her own person, and she was so content being herself that she only saw the good in everyone else. Her happiness bubble also made her fearless. I thought she was wonderful. After twelve miserable years of school, I was finally happy to be there.

One friend was all it took to turn the Hoover High gulag into someplace fun. It just took one Dahlia.

"My dad is getting my car painted next week," she told me while chewing on a mouthful of Chex Mix. "The color is 'Lavender Night.' It's got glitter in it. Doesn't that sound dreamy?"

"A car sounds dreamy," I said. It had been so long since I had even ridden in a car. I had to take two buses to get to the supermarket. I didn't know where my mom's car was. Cruz figured she sold it to have more money for Mexico.

I would have loved a car, even a glittery purple one.

"Let's go for a ride after school," Dahlia offered. "We could go to a place downtown I've heard of where Beat poets perform while you get your hair dyed. It's also supposed to serve kickass cappuccinos."

It sounded heavenly. All except the hair dye part. But I had to babysit after school, and I doubted I could afford Beat poetry and cappuccinos. I couldn't even afford Kraft mac-n-cheese.

"I can't. I'm babysitting today."

Dahlia cocked her head to the side, making a flood of curls flop over her left eye. "Maybe another day? I keep inviting you to stuff, but you never accept. Should I give up?"

No! Don't give up! A voice was screaming in my head, but I couldn't get it to come out of my mouth. I didn't want her to give up. I wanted her to be my best friend, and I wanted us to go all over town in her purple glittery car and have fun.

Just like other girls.

Just like I had always wanted.

But I didn't know how it was possible. Most of the time, she went to school parties where I wasn't welcome. She couldn't seem to understand that I wasn't a popular girl like her. And that wasn't the worst thing. The worst thing was: What if she found out that my mother had skipped the country and left me behind without any money?

Dahlia snapped her head back to center and blew a thick

curl off her face. "I'm not going to give up," she said, smiling. "Besides, I have something lined up that you can't refuse."

I got a lump in my throat, and I tried to swallow. I was afraid of not being able to refuse.

The school bell rang. "Don't be afraid," Dahlia said. "It's something you're going to really like."

I arrived home early that Friday at around 5:00. Babysitting had been a breeze. The Maclaren triplets had slept two hours, which allowed me to get most of my homework done. So, I was in a great mood when I walked up the path to my front door.

My open front door.

Cruz was standing on the front porch wearing a bathing suit and nothing else. He looked a lot like a Greek statue. The hard solid, marble kind of statue, perfectly proportioned in yum. His hair blew in the breeze, and his chest rose and fell with heavy breathing.

I still got waves of urges to lick him, but so far I had held back. Right about then I was battling a pretty strong licking urge. It was a toss up who was going to win. But the fact that Cruz wasn't alone put the odds on my side.

Our landlord was standing on the porch with him, and I didn't think he was there for a social visit. Cruz's arms were crossed in front of his chest, probably to keep himself from punching out our landlord, who was wagging his finger in Cruz's face and hollering at him.

"Who the hell are you?" the landlord asked him.

"I already explained, Mr. Stevens. I'm a friend of the family."

"Lord, that woman is going young!"

"It's not like that," Cruz explained. He grinned, which I knew meant that he was embarrassed. I would be, too, if I was him and I was accused of dating my mother.

"Hi, Mr. Stevens," I said, interrupting the conversation. "It's me, Tess."

He blinked a couple times, as if he was trying to reboot his brain and remember who I was. I detected a glimmer of recognition in his eyes and then relief.

"Where's your mother?" he demanded.

"Well—" I started. I caught Cruz throwing me a warning look. I had to be careful. If our landlord realized my mother had taken off without even leaving her contact information, he would call the cops, and I would wind up in a foster home.

My heart pounded in my chest. I was sure they could hear it. *Thump. Thump.* It was like the Marines Marching Band in there. How could they not hear it? I was a one-person rave.

I tried to calm myself enough to think of an excuse for my mom's disappearance. Where could she be? On retreat? At a spa? On a secret mission to Afghanistan? What would the landlord believe?

Thump. Thump. My heart wouldn't slow down. I couldn't get words out. I tried to remember the symptoms of a heart attack. Were sweating, panicking, and a heart on the verge of exploding symptoms? I was either having a heart attack, or I was the drummer for Kiss.

I opened my mouth and willed words to come out.

Nothing.

Not a peep.

Faced with the terror of being homeless, I forgot how to speak. Mr. Stevens didn't care, anyway. He wasn't interested in giving me a chance to explain.

"Do you know you're three months behind in the rent?" he demanded, his voice rising an octave. He sounded a lot like the Wicked Witch of the West, and I was half-expecting him to send flying monkeys after me.

"Three months?" Cruz asked.

"Three months?" I repeated, finally getting words out.

Cruz and I looked at each other. His face reflected my emotions.

Surprise.

Sadness.

Defeat.

My mother only left a month ago. We expected to be a month behind, but not three. How could we get three months of rent together?

"How much is the rent?" Cruz finally asked.

"Twelve-hundred a month. What's it to you, boy?"

I had saved two-hundred, and I knew that Cruz had just gotten his first paycheck.

"We can give you seven hundred and the rest next week," Cruz said.

"All twenty-nine-hundred?" the landlord asked.

Two thousand, nine hundred dollars. It was an impossible amount of money. He might as well have said a million dollars or a billion dollars. He might as well have said he needed me to turn my head all the way around or do the splits on a crate of dynamite.

I mean, impossible.

We could never get that much money together. We would have to win the lottery, invent Twitter, or get a Hip Hop contract to get that much money.

Tears burned the back of my eyes, threatening to pop out in a steady stream. I knew I would start blubbering any second. Faced with being a homeless orphan with their future flushed down the toilet, who wouldn't blubber?

I was about to drop to my knees, clutch onto the front of Mr. Stevens' Dockers, and beg him to let us live in the house for free, when Cruz said something crazy.

"Yep, twenty-nine-hundred," he said, although his voice was a little croaky, like it was hard for him to speak the actual words. Of course it was hard for him to speak the actual words! They were crazy words. Only a lunatic would say those words.

A lunatic who was convinced he had been abducted by aliens from Jupiter and had to learn their alien Jupiter language would hear Cruz say, "Yep, twenty-nine-hundred," and think: Blook bluck fep, which in Jupiter language means, "Those are crazy words!"

I flicked my eyes towards him, urging him to take back his crazy, but he wouldn't look at me.

The landlord didn't seem convinced at first, but just like everyone else who are willing to believe all kinds of baloney to make their lives easier, he latched onto Cruz's promise and nodded. "Okay. Where's the seven-hundred?"

I sprinted upstairs, dug my cookie tin from under my bed and emptied it. Cruz ran into in his room, and I heard a drawer open and close. We met at the top of the stairs, both holding fistfuls of cash.

"I'm sorry," I said.

"I'm sorry," he said.

We ran downstairs and handed the landlord his money. He counted it twice. "Next week," he said, sticking his finger in Cruz's face.

"Next week," Cruz agreed.

We stood on the front porch and watched the landlord walk down the front path, open his car door, get in, close the door, start the engine, and drive away. When he turned the corner at the end of the street and we were sure that he would leave us alone for at least a week, we walked back into the house and collapsed onto the bottom stair, sitting side by side.

"Cruz—"I started.

"I'll get it," he said.

"But—"

"I'll get it," he repeated.

The landlord's visit was a reminder of the barbarians at the gate. The ever-present danger. We had been fooling ourselves, thinking that we could make this work. We had slipped into an almost comfortable routine where I went to school and babysitting, and Cruz went to work and modeling auditions, and we would come home, make canned tomato soup, and then I would write in my notebooks, and he would go out with his beautiful friends.

Safe.

At least I had thought we were safe. It hadn't seemed to matter that we were throwing away bills and we hadn't heard a peep from our parents. But now, reality hit me like a ton of bricks. Like a landlord wearing Dockers and a short-sleeved buttoned down striped shirt.

"This will never work," I said on the step. I hadn't meant to say anything. I didn't want to be Debbie Downer when Cruz was working so hard to help me.

"We have no choice. It has to work."

"I was going to go to Paris and learn how to write," I said. This time the tears really did come. I wiped my nose on the hem of my t-shirt and sniffed.

Cruz turned to face me and raised his eyebrow. "I know. I think that's great."

He had beautiful eyes. Big, brown, and soft, like I could snuggle up inside them.

"I can't go to Paris," I said. "I don't have any money. How will I get there? How will I pay for the school?"

"Why do you want to go to Paris?" He asked the question as if he really wanted to know. He was interested in my thoughts and feelings, which still came as a surprise to me.

"Paris is everything I'm not," I said. "Beautiful, exciting, sophisticated. All the greatest writers have lived there."

"I can see you becoming a great writer."

"You can?"

"Yes," he said smiling ear to ear. "You'll be very famous, and you won't talk to me anymore. You'll only hang around your famous writer friends. You won't even take my calls."

It was ludicrous. I would always talk to him, if he let me. He was the perfect one, the one destined to be rich and famous. Couldn't he see that someday he would be the one to forget about *me*?"

"Your calls? You'll call me?" I asked.

"Or write letters. You being a writer and all, maybe you would prefer letters." I would love letters. I had never written an actual letter to anyone.

"Letters would be great," I said.

Cruz smiled. "Let's find something to eat."

He helped me up and put his arm around me as we walked to the kitchen. "You're such an idiot." He laughed.

"I am?"

"Yes. You were totally wrong."

"About what?" I asked.

"You're exactly like Paris."

There was nothing in the kitchen. We had eaten every last can of soup, every box of mac-n-cheese. We had run out of food and run out of money.

"I think this is how the Donner Party started," I said.

Cruz had the refrigerator door open, and he was staring inside it, as if he expected something to magically appear.

"Is your mother a member of Costco?" he asked.

"Yes, but we can't afford Costco."

"Did she leave her card here?"

Her Costco card was in the utility drawer. We took the bus to Costco and flashed the card to get in.

"When are you going to tell me what we're doing here?" I asked him. I have to admit I thought he planned to rob Costco. I was imagining him pretending to have a gun in his pocket and ordering them to hand over a giant bag of rice, a twelve-pack of tuna cans, and a six pound package of ground beef. It wasn't the most logical place to commit a robbery.

"We're going to eat," he said. "We're going to sample."

It was Friday evening, and Costco was packed with people and packed with employees handing out free samples. We pushed our cart to the first sample lady, who was handing out cheese and crackers. I ate two, and she gave us a dirty look.

"Do you think they're on to us?" I asked Cruz. We didn't look like typical Costco shoppers. First off, we were teenagers.

"We have to fit in. Put that box of Cheez Its into the cart."

I threw the box in, and just like that we looked like Costco shoppers. We circled the entire store, throwing whatever our hearts desired into the cart. Soda, cookies, pasta, and socks. We filled our cart like millionaires preparing for a nuclear holocaust. It was great to pretend that we had enough money to pay for it all.

In between our fake shopping, we sampled everything. We ate chips and salsa, hot wings, burritos, and cheesecake. We nibbled on egg rolls, brownies, and pulled pork. After we hit all the sample tables, we made another tour around the store.

An hour later, we were stuffed, and so was our cart. We stashed it in the aisle with the golf bags and bicycles and skipped out, expecting them to run after us and arrest us for sampling under false pretenses.

We ran through the parking lot and burst out laughing when we got to the bus stop. "That was the best meal I've had in ages," I said, trying to catch my breath from all the laughing.

"If I had had any money, I would have bought a bag of wings," he said, wistfully.

"You ate six of them."

"I couldn't get enough."

The bus arrived, and Cruz took my hand. At his touch, I felt my insides melt like ice cream on a hot day. We flashed our bus passes to the driver, and we took a seat near the back. Cruz didn't let go of my hand, and I noticed that all the women on the bus checked him out as he walked by.

Every female wanted him, but he didn't seem to notice them. He was with me.

"Tell me more about Paris and writing," he said.

I did. All the way home, sitting together and holding hands, our bellies full and forgetting that we needed three thousand dollars by next week, I told Cruz about Paris and writing.

I told him about Hemingway and F. Scott Fitzgerald. About Gertrude Stein and the Café de Flore. I told him about the

Sorbonne. Then I told him that I had been writing stories since I learned to write my name. How crafting a story was like breathing for me.

How writing was essential to live.

Cruz hung on every word. He leaned toward me, his face only inches from mine, studying my eyes and my mouth as I spoke. He was captivated by every detail, not bored at all by my dreams. I had never told anybody what I told Cruz that day on the bus. With every hope and goal and desire pouring out of me, they became even bigger, just by sharing them with Cruz.

He made my dreams more important, if only because he thought they were worthy. He also thought they were attainable.

"You're going to do it," he breathed. "You're going to do all of it."

We walked home from the bus stop, hand in hand. The street lights turned on, and a gentle breeze blew. In that moment, I was truly happy, and I felt for the first time in my life that everything I wanted was possible.

We arrived back home, and it seemed so had everyone else. The curb in front of the house was crowded with parked cars.

"There he is," announced a beautiful man in a gray suit. It was like Vogue magazine had thrown up all over our street. At least fifteen models were there, waiting for Cruz.

"Where have you been?" his friend Eric asked him.

"I was out shopping with Tess," Cruz said.

They noticed me for the first time, surprised that I was there. I had gone from being the center of Cruz's attention to the invisible girl, again.

"Get dressed," Dana ordered Cruz. "We're heading over to Bump for drinks and dancing."

The mob of models herded Cruz inside the house and got him prepared for their night out. When they were done, they paraded him downstairs. He was gorgeous, of course, dressed in tight black slacks and a fitted shirt. His hair was gelled, and he smelled delicious.

"I'll be back by midnight," he said to me, as he walked to the front door.

"Not if I have anything to say about it," said one of the models. I had seen her before. Blond, tall, rail thin, and perfectly beautiful. She took Cruz's face in her hands and kissed him long and hard.

They stayed like that for a minute, grinding against each other and swapping spit. I could see their tongues battling it out with each other when they opened and closed their mouths like big mouth bass or opera singers.

I felt my face go hot, and I wished to be really, truly invisible, to disappear into the floor and never return.

When they finally broke off their kiss, Cruz wrapped his

arm around her and she nestled her head on his shoulder. They walked out that way, like they were born for each other, leaving me with my dreams slightly battered, and my possibilities minus one.

Chapter 8

If I can stop one heart from breaking, I shall not live in vain.

--Emily Dickinson

There was a whole string of beautiful models who stuck their tongues down Cruz's throat. A different one every night. Sometimes groups of them.

I hate models.

Every stick-thin, cellulite-less, clear skinned, hair-extensioned, long-legged, well-dressed model.

Slightly less than Nazis but a whole lot more than brussels sprouts... Hate.

Here's what I learned about models while I lived with Cruz. First of all, they don't eat. I mean, nothing. I thought the up side to having the house invaded by swarms of twenty-somethings watching TV and gossiping was that they would at least bring chips and dip or a bucket of fried chicken. But there was a logical reason why they were so skinny (and boy, were they skinny!). Calories didn't pass their lips.

I saw one freak out once because she had eaten too much lettuce, and she had a shoot the next day. No lie.

The other thing I learned about models is that they travel in packs, like wolves or Mormons. Sometimes it was only Eric and Dana, who took turns driving Cruz around, but they were inevitably joined by at least five other fashion divas.

They would spread out on the couches and chairs in the living room--their little tushies taking up three or four inches of space—with the TV on to an entertainment show like Fashion Police or TMZ, and they would gossip about people in the industry. They had terrifying stories about things that happened during shoots that wouldn't have been out of place in soap operas or Dexter.

It sounded like a horrible way to make a living. Starving and dealing with predatory and abusive producers, photographers, and casting directors didn't sound glamorous to me.

But they were glamorous. Always done up, put together, and beautiful.

And they loved being models. They loved being thin and fabulous and having their pictures taken.

Don't get me wrong. I wasn't sitting on the couches with them, soaking up their stories and asking for more. I wasn't watching Fashion Police or discussing Milan's fashion week with them. As far as they were concerned, I didn't exist, and as far as I was concerned, I didn't want them to know I existed.

They scared me.

It would have been ridiculous for me to sit with them. I wasn't in their league. I wasn't even in their solar system.

But they were in my house, and I would catch snippets of their conversations when I had to go through the living room to get to the kitchen or when I was walking downstairs, and I happened to hear their voices when I paused on the staircase. I might have even eavesdropped once or twice. Or pretty much every day.

It wasn't that I wanted to get to know them or join them or be like them. I just wanted to know what Cruz was saying and what they were saying to him. Was he truly one of them, or was he just fitting in so that he could become a model? I didn't know. He was one person with them and another with me. But lately he was less and less with me.

After they hobnobbed on the couch, they inevitably went out clubbing. In a month, they had already made the rounds among the hottest clubs in Southern California. They were the barometer of hot clubs. I heard that the Kardashians followed *them* to find out which club was in.

The group of models was sort of incestuous, trading off girlfriends and boyfriends almost daily. I lost track of the girls' names who latched onto Cruz and let go just as suddenly. There were at least four Tiffany's and I don't know how many Summer's. So, I numbered them.

By November, I recognized numbers one through eighteen, gorgeous models that had slobbered all over Cruz, and he had slobbered all over them. I thought he was going to get serious with four, twelve, and sixteen, but he moved on after all of them.

Cruz never spoke about his women to me. Our conversations were limited to the house, eating, survival, and dreams. He didn't talk about his model friends and ditto about the landlord.

I never saw Mr. Stevens after that day on the front porch. I assumed Cruz got him his money, and I didn't know how that was possible. But if he didn't want to talk about it, I didn't want to ask him about it.

We were managing pretty well. The rent was paid, and the electricity was almost paid for. We were coming up to a shutoff date for our water, but I knew we could come up with enough money to keep it flowing. Otherwise, we ate peanut butter for almost every dinner. Cruz's model friends gave him designer clothes to wear, and I had a pretty large wardrobe of men's undershirts to keep me going.

As long as we didn't get sick or something didn't break, I thought we might make it. I was counting off the days until I graduated, and I think Cruz was doing the same. We had sort of given up on seeing our parents again.

Not that I missed my mother, but I wouldn't have minded her missing me, even just a little. I wouldn't have minded her calling me, even just once.

What can I say? Even a bad parent is a parent. I wanted one. I didn't know how many other kids had been abandoned by their mothers, but it wasn't probably that many. Deep inside me, I wondered if I didn't deserve to be abandoned, if my mother wouldn't have been a bad parent to a better daughter.

Besides that, I wondered about day-to-day problems. For instance, I was wondering if we were going to eat peanut butter for

Thanksgiving. The holiday was coming up fast, and I didn't care if I skipped a year of candied yams, but Thanksgiving also meant my college applications had to be done.

"Have you thought of Princeton? It's lovely," Mrs. Landes, the college advisor, told me, gently handing me a Princeton pamphlet, as if it was a priceless treasure.

Princeton? Who was she kidding?

True, I wanted to go the Sorbonne in Paris, which was a, who-am-I-kidding school, too. It was such a pipe dream, that I didn't dare tell her or anyone else that that's where I intended to go, and that's why I hadn't applied to any schools, yet.

I was already in the college advisor's office for over an hour, even though school ended forty-five minutes ago. Luckily, I didn't have babysitting today, but I could think of a million places I would rather be.

Mrs. Landes was at least three hundred years old and felt that every high school student should go on to college. It was a noble position to take, but at Hoover High, she was rolling that optimistic boulder up a steep hill.

She had been after me for weeks to come in and see her. "Do you realize you haven't applied anywhere?" she asked me in the hall. "Do you realize you still haven't taken the SAT?"

She hounded me until I couldn't say no any longer.

"You're such a good student," she said, taking the Princeton pamphlet back. "Normally good students are excited about college."

"I'm excited," I said, but my voice came out in a whisper, which was hardly an excited kind of voice.

"Don't you want to go to college?"

"Well—"

"It's hard to make a living without a college education these days," she said. "Besides, you're smart. You want to learn." Mrs. Landes leaned back in her rolling chair, making a creaking sound. "You do want to learn, don't you?"

It was kind of a do or die moment. Yes, I wanted to learn. I wanted to learn to write. And I wanted to do it in Paris, France while I wore a beret, ate croissants, and drank café au lait. It was my ultimate dream, what I had been waiting for years.

Impossible.

They would never accept me. I could never get there. I had no money. I couldn't afford the croissants and café au lait, let alone the plane ticket to France.

I felt ridiculous. I couldn't tell Mrs. Landes what I wanted. My mouth wouldn't work. It was like someone glued my lips together. There was no way I could tell her I wanted to be a writer and study in Paris. She would laugh at me. She would think I was delusional and call the white coats to take me to the funny farm where I would be locked away in a room with mattresses on the walls. She would point at me and tell me I was a crazy dreamer. Crazy. Nobody else at Hoover High wanted to go to the Sorbonne.

I was odd.

I was strange.

I was fooling myself.

"I want to be a writer," I said, finally. "And I want to study in Paris."

I gasped in surprise. What did I say? Where did those words come from? It was like someone was talking for me. It was like my mouth had a life of its own. And even more surprising, it wasn't finished. The words kept flowing.

"I want to go to the Sorbonne, even though I don't speak French. I want to be just like Hemingway and Gertrude Stein. I want to write books. Lots of books. Books that win prizes; books that people want to read. I never want to stop writing. I want to write in the Notre Dame cathedral, in the café de flore. I want to write everywhere in Paris.

"And yes, I want to learn. I want to learn how the words fit together, how to convey emotion, how to make people laugh and cry and want to turn the page. I want it all. Mrs. Landes, I want everything. But I can't afford the Sorbonne or a plane ticket to France or an apartment in Paris. I can't afford food. I can't afford any college, not even community college. I don't have money, and my mother has made it perfectly clear that she will never help me. She doesn't even believe in college."

I said it all in one big breath, and with the words finally out of me, I gasped for air. I flinched and shut my eyes, waiting for Mrs. Landes to start laughing or yell at me for being a really stupid girl.

But she didn't laugh. She didn't yell. In fact, she didn't say a word.

I slowly opened one eye to see if she had left the office. Nope. She was still there, sitting across from me with a big smile planted on her ancient face. She wore bright red lipstick that escaped her lips in little craggy lines. Her eyelids were painted blue and drooped over her eyes. She wasn't an attractive woman, but that was almost a relief since I had been surrounded by too much beauty, lately.

"I think that's a perfect idea," she said, finally.

"What?"

"You're going to go the Sorbonne in Paris and write great novels. I think that's the best idea I've heard in a long time."

"You do?"

"Don't you?" she asked me.

"Well—"

"You mustn't be wobbly, Tess. Dreams remain dreams if you get wobbly. It should be full steam ahead. Man the torpedoes." She shook her fist at the sky and bounced up and down in her chair, making it creak.

"The torpedoes?"

"Tell me what you've done so far."

"Done?"

"To get in. How's the application process going?"

Application process? What was she talking about? Hadn't she heard me? I didn't have any money. There was no way I could go to Paris.

Mrs. Landes cocked her head to the side. "You went away there, Tess. Come back to me. Focus."

I was focusing. Focusing on how impossible my dream was. Wobbly? I was so wobbly I had already fallen over.

"I can't go to Paris, Mrs. Landes."

"Why not?"

"I can't afford it."

"Stuff and nonsense."

"Stuff and what?" I asked.

"Balderdash. Claptrap. Twaddle. Tripe. Drivel. Of course you can go to Paris."

"But—" I started.

"No buts. You're going to research everything about studying at the Sorbonne, and so am I, and then we're going to meet back here on Tuesday during fifth period. Got it?" She penciled my name on her desk calendar and waved me out of the room.

I stood outside the office and took a deep breath. It was warm for November, and there wasn't a cloud in the sky. I felt a kernel of hope pop inside me. Could I really make my dreams come true? Could I really make it to Paris, after all?

For the first time in a long time I was optimistic, but the optimism wasn't alone. It was kept company by a big dose of fear. There's nothing scarier than hoping for something and not getting it.

On the other hand, Mrs. Landes seemed very sure. She wasn't scared at all. And more than that, she didn't laugh at me. In fact, she thought it was a great idea. She told me I shouldn't be wobbly.

It dawned on me that my best choice for happiness rested in the hands of an old lady with droopy eyelids and red lipstick. That sort of made me happy.

I walked out of the college advisor's office to a quiet school and an empty quad. It was a long way across the campus to the exit. The nice weather and my new hope kept me company and made the walk enjoyable. I planned on getting on my mom's computer and researching everything I could the minute I got home. It was great to get permission to turn my dream into reality.

I walked through the school's front gate. There were only a few cars in the parking lot, but hovering at the entrance were about five kids, talking around a white Challenger. I recognized them: Three football players and two of the meanest of the mean girls.

I would have to pass them to walk through the lot toward home. I took a deep breath and scrunched up my courage. I knew it could go one of two ways. Either they would ignore the invisible girl, or they were bored and would use me as a distraction.

It turned out to be the second option.

"Look, it's the freak," one of the girls announced.

Their heads turned toward me in unison. It was like they were watching a tennis tournament, and I was the ball.

Great. Just perfect.

Two of the football players blocked me from passing them. They were huge, at least six-feet-tall with thick necks and bulging biceps.

"Where do you think you're going, freak girl?" One of them demanded. I think his name was Ralph, but he could just have as easily been called, Tank or Butch.

Or Killer.

Gulp.

"Who do you think you are, eating lunch every day with Dahlia?" A cheerleader demanded. "She doesn't want to sit with you, you know."

My breath hitched, and I choked back a tear. Could that be true? Dahlia really didn't want to sit with me? Is that what she told her cheerleader friends?

"I think freak girl is going to cry," Ralph said, obviously overjoyed.

"You're getting all your freak girl germs on Dahlia," the

cheerleader continued. "You're bringing her down. You get me?"

She punctuated her question with a shove. Two hands right to my chest. She was stronger than she looked, and I flew back a couple feet. The third football player got behind me and pushed me back in the other direction.

"Please..." I began, which made them laugh and seemed to spur the cheerleader into shoving me again.

It occurred to me that I might die there, beaten to death by the school's popular kids just as I had a glimmer of hope of making it to Paris. How typical.

Ralph spit in my face, and the cheerleader shoved me again, this time much harder, and I fell to the ground with the wind knocked out of me. I looked up into their faces and read the determination there. I started to really cry. Big tears streamed down my face. It wasn't so much the pain of being pushed down or the fear of being hurt that got me sobbing. It was the humiliation—a lifetime of humiliation culminating in this moment—that broke me. And I knew something else:

They weren't done.

They weren't close to done.

There was a loud popping noise, like a gun going off. I checked my body to see if I had been shot, but I was okay. The others turned around in the direction of the noise.

A tiny car with more dents than not came chugging into the parking lot. It had two doors and a crushed hood. It sounded like a wind-up toy when it moved. *Clack. Clack. Clack.* I wouldn't have been surprised if it had been put together with three paper clips and a rubber band.

It clacked right up to us, stopping just behind the Challenger. That's when I recognized the driver, and my heart skipped a beat.

And I died a little.

Died in a good way.

He either turned off the car, or it stopped running on its own. Either way the engine choked and sputtered until it was quiet. The driver's window slowly opened with a tortured squeal. He stuck his arm out and found the door handle, opening it from the outside with a creak. The door sort of dropped a couple inches when it was fully open, and I half-expected it to fall off altogether.

Cruz hopped out of the car. He was tall and built, handsome as ever in jeans and a t-shirt. He was also pleased as punch, his mouth stretched in an ear-to-ear smile that could stop traffic and rev girls' hearts for miles.

"Tess, look what I got!" he shouted with pride.

The popular kids turned toward me, and their faces said it all: shock, surprise. Why was the most beautiful, perfect boy on the planet talking to the invisible girl?

Cruz's face said it all, too, when he realized I was on the ground, surrounded by football players, my hair and clothes disheveled, and my cheeks most likely stained with tears. I had never seen his face like that: fighting mad.

Capable of murder.

Chapter 9

It is better to be the hammer than the anvil.

--Emily Dickinson

Cruz stared right at me, his eyes never wavering, as he made a beeline toward me. He elbowed the others out of his way until he reached me. He bent down, took my hands, and pulled me up.

"All you all right?" he asked, holding my hands with his face inches from mine. He spoke softly and clearly, his voice coming from deep in his chest and sounding ominously like a growl.

"Yes," I said and started to cry again. It was either the relief of seeing Cruz there or realizing what almost happened that made my emotions bubble up and spill over.

Cruz wiped the tears from under my eyes with his thumbs and held my head in his hands. He pulled me forward and he leaned down until our foreheads were touching. He closed his eyes and breathed deep.

In. Out. In. Out.

I didn't know if he was trying to calm himself or trying to build his energy.

After a few seconds his eyes flew open, and he stepped back, dropping his hands to his sides. He nodded and then faced my attackers.

"Who's responsible for this?" he demanded. "I want to know who I'm going to kill."

His threat was real. Waves of anger wafted off him. I'm sure I wasn't the only one who could feel the pure animal aggression crackling in the air like an electrical storm. Ralph shifted his weight from foot to foot, as if he was deciding which way to run. The two mean girls chewed on their lower lips and stepped backward.

But the other two football players stood their ground. They seemed to welcome the threat of a fight, and they probably reasoned—wisely--that two beats one, especially two giant football players against one thin, yet well-defined, model.

They were wrong.

Cruz marched over to the biggest football player and got in his face. They were about the same height, but the other guy was much bigger than Cruz.

"You are so dead," he told Cruz.

Cruz didn't respond. His hand formed into a fist. He cocked his arm back and let it fly into the football player's face. It landed with a crack that sent him flying backward into the Challenger. Blood shot out of his nose, as if a hose were turned on inside his brain.

I was sure Cruz had broken his hand, but he seemed unfazed and ready to knock out the next guy in line. The girls had run off with Ralph the second their friend's nose started to bleed, but the other guy was hopping in place, ready to fight nine rounds.

I clutched onto Cruz's arm. "Please," I said. "Stop. They're not worth it."

Cruz refocused his eyes, looking at me as if he had forgotten I was there and was surprised by my presence. "They're not worth it," he agreed. "But you are."

I stopped breathing. Time stood completely still. I looked around and saw everyone frozen in place: The bad guys ready to fight. Cruz, the good guy, who cared about me.

Was that right? Did he care about me?

I sucked in air and time moved on once more.

"I don't want you to get hurt," I told Cruz. "I don't want you to get into trouble."

I had visions of a dead and broken Cruz, of a Cruz in handcuffs on his way to jail. I couldn't bear the thought of him hurt or in trouble. And I couldn't bear the thought of being alone without him.

"Please," I repeated.

"Are you all right?" he asked me. "Did they hurt you?"

"No. Let's go home."

Cruz nodded, and that's when the football player sucker

punched him. Cruz pushed me out of the line of fire, and he ducked in time so that the punch didn't have much impact. Still, he would have a black eye in the morning. That was for sure.

If I had been Cruz, I would have run away crying, but he seemed fired up by getting hit. Without skipping a beat, he stomped on the football player's foot and punched him square in the stomach.

Everyone had had enough after that. The guy with the nosebleed jumped into the Challenger and started it up. The other guy hopped into the passenger seat, and they peeled away from the curb, racing out of the lot with their tires squealing.

Cruz and I stood in place and watched them go. We could hear them speeding in the distance long after we could no longer see their car.

I took Cruz's hand and inspected it for damage. His knuckles were cracked and dotted with blood.

"It's nothing, Tess."

"Can you move your fingers?"

"Of course I can," he said and opened and closed his fist several times to show me.

I touched his cheekbone. "How about your face? Are you in one piece?"

"He barely touched me. Don't worry. I'll still be beautiful."

He winked and smiled. I was so relieved that he was all right that I wrapped my arms around his waist and squeezed him tight. Just as I became aware that I was hugging a beautiful model who probably didn't want to be hugged by the likes of me, he hugged me back.

Cruz hugged me like I had always dreamed of being hugged. His arms wrapped around me, and he drew me even closer to him. The length of our bodies touched, and he rested his chin on the top of my head.

I don't know how long we stayed that way, but I never wanted to leave his embrace. I discovered that day that once I was in Cruz's arms, I never wanted to leave.

"Where did you get it?" I asked Cruz.

We stood next to the tiny car and studied it. It was worse close up. I couldn't believe it ran. It looked like it was a school project. Like it was made of paper mache and Elmer's glue.

"It was a gift," he said, smiling and obviously proud. "A free car."

"A free car? A car for free? Like no money kind of free?" I thought free cars were urban legends, like spider trees and solar flares. "Who gave you a car for free?"

"A friend of a friend. He said he didn't need it anymore."

There were streaks of rust on the car's roof, and the

taillights were broken and covered with red plastic.

"Imagine that. He didn't need it," I said.

"Now, now. Don't throw shade. It runs, and you know what this means?"

"What does it mean?"

"No more buses."

The inside made the outside look like a Bentley. The front seats were ripped and stained, which were better than the back seats because there weren't any back seats, discarded by the previous owner. It didn't have any floor mats either, and we could see right down to the rusty metal undercarriage.

"We're not going to fall through, are we?" I asked Cruz.

"I'm almost positive we won't."

"This car is street legal, right?"

"I'm almost positive it is."

Besides a steering wheel and a stick shift with no knob on the end, the inside was empty. No radio. No nothing.

"I don't think it has windshield wipers," I noted.

"Luckily it doesn't rain often in San Diego. This is called a choke," Cruz explained, pulling something next to the steering wheel. "You don't see these in cars nowadays." He turned the ignition, and the car started on the third try.

"Phew," he said. "I think I'm getting the hang of it. I flooded it twice before, but this time it started right up."

He pushed the choke back in, moved the stick shift into first gear, and the car jolted into motion. It clack, clack, clacked through the parking lot, occasionally burping and farting and finally letting out an explosive backfire when we got to the stop sign.

"See?" Cruz said. "It runs like a dream."

Cruz was intoxicated with the freedom that the car offered us. I was thrilled, too, even though I thought it would eventually fall apart completely and we would wind up stranded on the side of the road. But for now, I cranked open my window and enjoyed the ride.

"Where are we going?" I asked.

"To the beach."

"Which beach?"

"All of them."

He drove up and down the coast, at least one hundred miles of scenic roads. After being cooped up at home and at school without any money to do anything and a fear of being found out, the freedom was delicious.

Four wheels and an internal combustion engine provided endless possibilities. We could go wherever our hearts desired. We were free, free, free.

Just like the car but with wind in our hair.

Free.

"What kind of car is this?" I asked.

"I think it's Portuguese or Brazilian."

I let that soak in a bit. I didn't know anything about cars, but I was pretty sure Portugal and Brazil were not known for their automobiles.

"This thing gets amazing gas mileage," I noted.

"I know, right?"

I leaned over and looked at the gas gauge. "It still says it's full."

Cruz flicked the gas gauge with his finger. The needle didn't move. It still read that the tank was full even though we had gone at least one hundred miles.

"Did you fill it up today?" I asked.

"Fill it up?"

"You didn't fill it up?"

"It was already full when I got it," he said and tapped the gauge again. It didn't move. "Oh."

"Oh."

"Tess, I have a bad feeling about this."

As if on cue, the car sputtered and wheezed. Then it sort of died, its clacking, burping, and farting silenced. Cruz turned the steering wheel to the right, and we glided to the side of the road.

Out of gas.

"It was fun while it lasted," I said.

"I guess I shouldn't have assumed the gauge would work. I saw a gas station a couple blocks that way," he said pointing behind us. "We can get a gas can and then fill it up. Hey, you know, the beach is right here."

Across the street was a long stretch of beach, almost totally empty, and the sun was about to go down. A ribbon of pink stretched across the sky. It was a lovely evening.

"How about a picnic on the beach, and we could watch the sunset?" he asked.

It sounded heavenly. Like a dream. I was already planning on writing all about it in my notebook when I got home.

"I brought sandwiches," he said, as if he had to convince me to picnic with him on the beach. "Only peanut butter, though."

"I'd love to," I said.

Even though I had eaten a million peanut butter sandwiches during the past month, these were delicious and special, eating them while sitting on the beach with Cruz. He surprised me with Doritos, too.

"When did we get so rich?" I asked, holding up a chip.

"I decided every time we get a new car, we can splurge for

a bag of Doritos."

"Wow. Fancy."

The sunset put on quite a show for us. The evening sky was ablaze in pastel colors; as if it decided it wasn't going to go dark without a statement.

"I think things are looking up," Cruz said.

"I think so, too."

"I've got a casting tomorrow. Nothing major—just an online catalog–but it would be a good paycheck if I got it."

"That's awesome."

"I wish the modeling thing would happen quicker. It would help us out a lot."

Us. When he spoke about his dreams, it was about *us*. I never thought about us when I thought about my dreams. Cruz was definitely out of the picture when I imagined myself writing in Paris. Was there an *us*? Could I ever hope for an *us*? An *us* in Paris?

"Tess?" he asked.

"Yes?"

"You don't know how to drive, do you?"

My mother would never allow me to drive her car, so she didn't see much use in me getting a drivers permit or license. No parent permission equals no driver's license.

"You're looking at me funny," I said.

Cruz was crazy.

Nuts.

Cray-cray.

Certifiable.

I never thought I would say no to him. Not for anything. Not in a million years.

But no.

I mean…no.

"No!" I shouted, stomping my foot on the black top. I crossed my arms in front of me and scowled.

"It'll be fun. You'll see."

We had walked to the gas station, gotten a gas can, and filled up the car. Then Cruz sing-songed "I know what we're going to do," and drove through the night to the stadium on the other side of town.

The stadium was dark—no games tonight—but the parking lot was lit up and noisy. Race cars and regular cars were driving at breakneck speeds along a chalk-lined course.

Amateur drivers of all ages were either racing, waiting in or by their cars to race, or were hanging out with each other, drinking beers and waiting for their turns.

The roars of the engines and the squealing of the brakes filled the air. They were driving like maniacs. Most of them couldn't stay within the lines and would maneuver wildly to get back on track. Others steered straight into the fence. I saw two cars do that, and one had to be towed away.

"No!" I yelled again.

"It'll be fun. You have to learn to drive sometime."

He had a point. I did have to learn to drive sometime. At some point in my life, I would have enough money to buy a car, or maybe I would be like Cruz and get a free car, and then I would need to drive.

I had to admit that even Emily Dickinson would have learned to drive, if cars had been invented back then.

"No," I said.

"It'll be fun. Car racing. What's more fun than that? Don't you want to race my free car?"

I looked at his free car. Its side view mirror fell to the ground with a clank. Then I looked back at the racetrack. Two Porsche collided and spun into the fence.

"No."

"Tess." He looked deep into my eyes and put his hand on my shoulder. The instant he touched me a jolt of electricity went through my body. I swayed backward, and Cruz caught me. "Are you okay?"

No. I was definitely not okay. I looked away and covered my face with my hands. My cheeks were hot to the touch, which made sense, because it felt like my whole body was about to go up in flames. I made a humiliating gasping sound, like I was hyperventilating or doing a Zumba class.

"I was joking, Tess," Cruz said with concern in his voice. "I didn't expect you to drive on the track. I was going to teach you over there in the corner. You won't have to be near any of the racers. Tess?"

My hair had fallen over my face, and he gently tucked a thick strand behind my ear. "I'm sorry I teased you," he said, completely misunderstanding why I was upset.

I didn't correct him. I didn't want him to know that his touch could render me speechless. Breathless and gasping for oxygen. I didn't want him to know my feelings for him because it was obvious he didn't share the same feelings for me. If he did, he wouldn't be sticking his tongue down the throats of skinny, perfect models.

I finally regained control over myself, and I punched him in the arm.

"That's for scaring me half to death," I lied.

Cruz put his hands up in the air. "Sorry. Sorry. It won't happen, again."

I didn't learn to drive that day. In fact, I didn't learn to drive for years after. Instead, we sat in the free car in a dark corner of the noisy parking lot with me in the driver's seat. Cruz showed me the gas pedal and the turn signal, and I played at moving the stick shift.

"It's probably not safe for you to actually drive," he said.

"You finally figured that out?"

"You've mixed up the gas pedal with the brake pedal three times," he noted.

"Well they look exactly alike."

"I know. That can be confusing. Normally people tell them apart because the gas is on the right and the brake is in the middle."

"Ohhh..." I said. "Then what's this other pedal?"

"I think we should leave well enough alone and just make vroom vroom noises."

I laughed. "I think I can do that."

I never started the car. We bounced up and down, pretending we were driving down a bumpy road, and I steered and stepped on the pedals, not worrying which one was which. We pretended we were driving down the Champs-Élysées in Paris, along the autobahn in Germany, and through a giant sequoia in northern California. When we had had enough, we switched seats, and Cruz drove us home.

With no radio, and our conversation used up, the car was quiet during the ride back to the house. In the dark with Cruz's attention on the road ahead, I allowed myself to stare at him. It was like an artist had sculpted him. Like Michelangelo's David. He was beautiful, but I saw more than just his beauty.

I saw inside him and found my heart there.

Chapter 10

Beauty is not caused. It is.

--Emily Dickinson

The house was quiet, and Cruz had nowhere to go, for a change. We sat on the couch together and watched a black and white movie on TV while I did my homework. Senior year was a lot easier than junior year.

Last year it was all about proving ourselves, making the grades to get into college. This year was more relaxed at school. Less homework, fewer tests. Our stress was now centered on the college application process and wondering what our futures would hold.

That was plenty of stress, believe you me.

December first had come and gone, and there was still no word from our parents. It was like they had forgotten they had kids. I pictured them living in a luxury resort on the beach in Mexico, sipping Mai Thais. I could envision my mother lying on the beach saying to The Boyfriend: "Have I forgotten something? Oh, well. Must not be important."

Either that or they were dead.

Or in Jail.

Or they never existed, and I made her up.

I mean, anything was possible. Since I had no idea how to reach them, I guessed I would never know.

"Six more months," Cruz mumbled.

"What?"

He turned down the TV. "I was just thinking out loud. We have six more months until you graduate and I leave for my modeling. We can stop paying bills at the end of March and ride it out through June. They won't kick us out before then. Anything we make for those two and a half months we can save. Do you understand?"

I nodded. I had been living day to day and hoping for the best, but Cruz had been doing real planning. He was organizing everything around my graduation.

"What do you mean leave for your modeling?" I asked.

"Eric is going to get me work in Japan. A lot of male models make their start there."

"Oh." It was the first time I heard about Japan. I got queasy thinking about him leaving, going far away from me. But wasn't that what I wanted to do, as well? I planned on going halfway around the world, too. And then something else dawned on me.

"Cruz," I said. "If you can go in June, couldn't you go now?"

"Oh, no," he said, not looking at me in the eyes. "It's

better to wait. I can get more pictures taken for my portfolio in the meantime, and besides, Japan is cold in the winter."

It was a flimsy excuse. I knew he was lying. He was obviously waiting around in order to take care of me. And I was selfish enough not to fight him on it. I would never make it at home without Cruz. He was giving me a huge gift by sticking around for another six months, putting off his career all that time. He was saving my life.

He was also counting on me to graduate in six months and be alright to go to France with some way of supporting myself. But how could I make that happen? Mrs. Landes, the college advisor, hadn't found a scholarship that would pay for my plane ticket and my housing in Paris.

I had filled out an application to the Sorbonne with her help, but I didn't know if I would be accepted. There were so many things that could go wrong. There was so much riding against me.

"Yes, I hear Japan is cold in the winter," I said.

"I hate the cold."

"Me, too. At least I think I do." I had never been outside of San Diego, and the city wasn't known for cold winters.

I finished my homework and closed my books. The movie on TV caught my attention. It was an old comedy with Katherine Hepburn and Cary Grant.

"You're like that," Cruz said.

"What did you say?" I turned to see him studying me, like I was a puzzle. He didn't blink; His eyes were deep and fathomless and drew me in.

"You're like Katherine Hepburn. Classy. Smart."

I was slightly stunned, but I was woken out of my stupor by the doorbell. We both assumed it would be for Cruz. Who else would it be for?

He hopped off the couch, answered the door, and came back into the living room.

"It's for you," he told me. "Your friend."

"My what?"

"Your friend! Your best friend!" Dahlia announced, skipping into the room. She danced around Cruz and plopped onto the couch next to me. She was wearing a man's pinstripe suit, and her hair was French braided and twisted into a bun. She carried a large clear, plastic purse, and I could see a box of Pop Tarts among her makeup, papers, wallet, and other stuff. She kicked off her sandals and crossed her legs on the couch.

I had felt awkward near Dahlia since the incident at school with the cheerleaders and football players. I couldn't forget what they said about Dahlia not really wanting to hang out with me. I didn't know if it was true or not, but I thought I should try to give her some space. So, I had been avoiding her at lunchtime, making excuses that I had to go to the library or study hall. I didn't want to lose such a good friend, but I didn't want her talking about how annoying I was, either.

"Oh, I love this movie!" Dahlia announced. "It's one of my favorites."

On TV, Katherine Hepburn had ripped the back of her dress and was walking around a restaurant with the back of her underwear showing. I could totally see Dahlia doing the same thing, and I started to giggle.

Dahlia laughed, too. "Oh, I'm so glad to see you!" she said. "It's been so long. You've been way too busy so I figured if the mountain won't go to Dahlia, well you know."

She had gotten the saying a little mixed up, but it didn't matter. I was happy. She obviously wanted to see me, and those cheerleading finks were big fat liars. Or skinny little liars.

They were bitches.

"You'll never guess what I brought," she said.

"Pop Tarts."

"Wow! How did you guess?"

I didn't point out that her purse was see-through. She opened the box and handed me a foiled package. I ripped it open and took a bite.

"And who are you?" she asked Cruz, who sat down on the other side of me. "No, let me guess. You're Chino."

She smiled, and I blushed. Dahlia offered Cruz some Pop Tarts, but he refused since he had to stay a certain size for modeling.

I didn't need to stay a certain size. I purposefully wore clothes that were a size too big so I could go up and down depending on my craving for carbs and the time of the month. Right then, I was PMSing pretty bad, and if a doctor was around, I was sure he would prescribe a big dose of Pop Tarts. Besides, they were s'mores flavored. My favorite.

"I'm not going to ask what's going on here," Dahlia said, pointing from me to Cruz. "I believe that would be a karmic violation, and I'm not willing to do that while I'm waiting to hear back from Smith College. My father wants me to go to Brown, but Sylvia Plath went to Smith. You know?"

I didn't know if it was all that prudent to follow in Sylvia Plath's footsteps. Besides, Dahlia wanted to be a math major.

"I'm Cruz," he said shaking her hand.

"I'm Dahlia. Tess's biggest admirer. Or am I? Maybe I'm her second biggest admirer?" She arched her eyebrow and cocked her head at Cruz. My face got hot, but Cruz's face looked like it was the Hindenburg landing. On fire. He was a red, ripe tomato.

Dahlia didn't seem to notice. She bit into a Pop Tart and slapped my knee. "I have big news for you. Big!"

She was wearing inch long fake eyelashes, which were purple and glittery—I think to match her new car—and her hair was tied in a top knot, which looked like a blond toilet paper roll was glued to the top of her head. I was slightly afraid of her 'big news.'

She opened her purse and rifled through it. "I know it's here somewhere." She pulled out a couple dirty Kleenex, a curling iron, and finally an envelope, which she held up with an air of victory. "Voila! And notice I said that in French." She winked at me, and her purple eyelashes stuck together.

I helped her upstairs to my bathroom, and she washed the eyelashes off. "I was half-hoping it wouldn't unstick, and I could have an eye patch," she said with her face in the sink. "I have a great scarf to tie around my head, and it would be fabulous to pull off a whole pirate look."

Dahlia dried off, and I quickly hung up all of Cruz's wet towels. She took the envelope, and I showed her my bedroom. She went right for the floppy hat on my dresser.

"Love this. *Love* this!" she cried, trying it on. "Do I look like Scarlett O'Hara?"

She looked nothing like Scarlett O'Hara. First of all, her giant top knot prevented the hat from sitting on her head. It just bobbed there, as if Dahlia had become a walking hat stand.

She looked around my room, taking a moment over my stacks of notebooks. Then she sat on my bed, and patted the place next to her. "Come and open it, already," she said.

I sat down, and she gave me the envelope. I couldn't imagine what it was. I opened it, careful not to rip the fancy linen paper.

"You're invited to my family's Christmas party," she announced before I could read the invitation. "It's on the eighteenth. So not strictly Christmas, but you get the picture. There will be lots of green and red, and food. Food, Tess!

Mushroom caps and lobster puffs, and oodles of good things. Please say you'll come. Please! And you can sleep over. I'm so excited you're coming. It will be so much more fun with you there. Normally it's only family and their stuffy friends, but my father said I could invite you. We're going to have the best time!"

"What's a lobster puff?" I asked.

I had never been to a Christmas party, let alone one with lobster puffs. I had no idea what a lobster puff was, but I bet it was fancy. Christmas party dress fancy. What on earth would I wear? What would I say to everyone? They would talk about international affairs, the stock market, and opera. What could I contribute to that conversation? I could talk about surviving on peanut butter sandwiches and hoping the water wasn't shut off in the house.

Or I could talk about my mother abandoning me.

No. Probably not a topic for a lobster puff party.

"Well—" I started. I didn't want to let her down. She really did want me to go, but she didn't know what she was asking. I would be out of place at her fancy party that required linen paper invitations. I wasn't that kind of person. She would see that I was an outsider, and never want to be my friend again. I mean, I didn't even know what a lobster puff was. Wasn't that a red flag for her?

"Good!" Dahlia hugged me, and I flinched. I had so seldom been hugged in my life, it felt weird. But good. "Don't forget your surprise," she whispered in my ear. "It's coming soon."

I couldn't imagine what my surprise would be. I thought finding out what lobster puffs were would be surprise enough.

After ten that night, Dahlia decided to go home. Cruz offered to walk her out to her car, and I watched them from my bedroom window, making out their shadows in the moonlight. They were talking and laughing. Dahlia pulled keys from her purse and leaned back against the side of her car. She was very pretty, and she was self-confident without being a conceited egomaniac like other girls. Her face was just like a doll's or a Disney princess. She could obviously have any boy she wanted, and I was struck with a pang of jealousy.

I was about to step away from the window and get ready for bed when I saw Cruz step closer to her. She stopped smiling. I could imagine the tension between them, being so close to each other.

And then his mouth touched the side of her face.

I grew cold, as if an arctic wind had hit me. I squinted and looked again to make sure I hadn't hallucinated. But by then it was too late. Cruz had hopped back on the curb, and Dahlia was sitting in her car, starting it up. I heard the front door slam when Cruz walked inside the house. Dahlia's headlights turned on, and she raced down the street with the soft sound of her car's Katy Perry music reaching me.

I tried to swallow, but a large lump in my throat prevented me. Tears burned the back of my eyes, and my nose ran, dripping two drops on the carpet. I had seen Cruz kiss lots of pretty girls, lots of beautiful women, but seeing him with my only friend broke my heart into pieces like a cracker at the bottom of a box.

Dust.

It was a writing moment, a time to write my guts out in one of my notebooks. The urge to write out every detail of my pain and those that inflicted that pain gnawed at me, but my body had grown heavy. I had a hard time moving at all.

With my last bit of energy, I changed into my nightgown and got into bed. I turned on my side, away from the light of the hallway and tried to close my eyes. As tired as I was, however, my eyes wouldn't shut, and I couldn't fall asleep.

"Psst. Tess, you asleep?" I turned over. Cruz was standing in the doorway, his body outlined in the light from the hall. "Do you mind if I stay with you a little while?"

You wouldn't think having a beautiful boy ask if he could stay with you for a little while would make a girl cry, but that's what happened. Luckily, it was a quiet cry. No sobbing. No choking or gasping for breath. Just a few tears streaming down my face.

I didn't want him to know I was crying, and I didn't trust my voice. So, I patted the place on the bed next to me instead of saying anything. He kicked off his shoes and hopped on. He wore shorts and a t-shirt, and he smelled like apples and sunlight.

"I can't go to sleep, yet," he said, softly. "I hope you don't mind. I always feel calmer when I'm with you."

I never felt calm when I was with Cruz. I always felt like my blood was racing through my veins. Now with him lying next to me, our bodies almost touching, my blood was doing a pretty decent NASCAR impression.

"Tell me a story," he urged. "You're the story writer. Tell

me one to help me sleep."

"One of mine?" I asked. I had never read my stories to a soul.

Cruz and I lay on our sides, our faces only about an inch apart. I could smell his breath—sweet and warm, and I could just make out his big brown eyes staring back at me.

"You scared?" he asked.

"Scared?" Damn right I was scared. I was scared I was going to jump all over him and make a fool of myself. Or worse.

"Yeah, you know, scared of reading one of your stories," he said. "Okay, how about a different story, maybe from one of your favorite writers."

"Well, my favorite writer is Emily Dickinson, but she was a poet."

"A poet," he repeated. I inhaled his words, his breath invading my body, mingling with my own. "Tell me one of her poems. Do you know one by heart?"

I knew a lot of her poems by heart. She was my constant companion.

I nodded. "But you don't want to hear it," I said.

Cruz caressed my cheek with the tip of his finger. "Tell me," he said, softly. My skin sprouted goose bumps, and I shivered.

"Okay, but I warned you. It's not Stephen King."

"THE WAY I read a letter's this:
'T is first I lock the door,
And push it with my fingers next,
For transport it be sure.

And then I go the furthest off
To counteract a knock;
Then draw my little letter forth
And softly pick its lock.

Then, glancing narrow at the wall,
And narrow at the floor,
For firm conviction of a mouse
Not exorcised before,

Peruse how infinite I am
To—no one that you know!
And sigh for lack of heaven,—but not
The heaven the creeds bestow.'"

I finished reciting the poem. Silence. Not a peep out of the hunky, dreamy eyed, perfect boy on my bed. It was the kind of silence a brain makes when it's trying to figure out something nice to say.

Obviously, Cruz couldn't figure out something nice to say.

"I told you it wasn't Stephen King," I said. I was sweating embarrassment out of my pores. I knew I shouldn't recite an Emily Dickinson poem. What was I thinking? No boy is going to like Emily Dickinson. And now I would be even less cool, even less of one of his beautiful models, even more of a dork.

"You have a beautiful voice," he said finally.

"I do?"

"So full of passion when you were talking. I didn't know what it meant, but it was beautiful."

I pinched myself. Yep, I was awake.

"It was," I croaked. "about letters. Receiving letters, I mean. Back in those days they wrote lots of letters."

"I've never written anybody an actual letter," said Cruz. "Not with a pen on paper and mailing it in a mailbox."

"Me either. And I've never gotten one."

Cruz sighed, deeply, and I inhaled his breath, again.

"It must be nice, though, taking the time to write it out slowly by hand. Then, mailing it and waiting a long time for an answer. It's more thoughtful than a text or email. It's sort of romantic. You probably think I'm a dork," he said.

"What? No!"

"Probably your boyfriends don't talk about writing letters."

My boyfriends.

My boyfriends?

Was Cruz on crack? What was he talking about? The closest I had ever gotten to having a boyfriend was right that second, lying in bed with him. And for sure, Cruz wasn't my boyfriend. He was too busy kissing models and my best friend to be my boyfriend.

"I would love to get a letter," I said, sidestepping the whole boyfriend conversation.

"Maybe when I'm in Japan and you're in France, we could write back and forth. You know, the old fashioned way."

It was a nice thought, but I bet Cruz would forget about me when he was modeling all over the world.

"Are you excited about going to Japan?" I asked.

"Nervous."

I yawned. It had gotten awfully late, and Cruz's voice was soft and deep, and lulled me. "You're going to be great," I said. "Famous. Rich."

My eyes flickered closed, and I dozed off. Cruz took my hand, and he slipped his body under the covers. His breathing grew heavy, and I knew he was drifting off, too. Right before I fell asleep, I heard him say:

"By the way, don't use the pool anymore. We can't afford

chlorine."

We woke up the next morning together in bed. In the light of day, our situation grew awkward. We had gotten tangled in the blankets, our limbs intertwined. If someone walked into my bedroom at that moment, they would have thought all kinds of things.

Awkward things.

Our eyes locked and something passed between us unsaid, which I didn't totally understand. Connection. And it came with a tension that I knew we both felt.

And then it was gone. In a blink of an eye, Cruz broke the connection, hopped up from my bed, and raced out of my room.

In that instant, it changed. We changed. On some level, I knew that we had embarked on a path that we couldn't alter. I didn't know, however, that we would travel it together.

Chapter 11

Not knowing when the dawn will come I open every door.

--Emily Dickinson

Living in Southern California, birthday parties mean piñatas. My whole life I never had a piñata for my birthday, but when I was invited to birthday parties back in elementary school and it was my turn to whack the piñata, I would take the baseball bat and go all A-Rod on its ass.

Home run. Candy everywhere.

I love candy.

So, believe it or not, I wasn't suspicious one bit when Dahlia offered to drive me home from school and there was a Smurf piñata lying on her backseat. Yes, I was suspicious about the ride home. She had never given me a ride home before, and I didn't really want her around Cruz after the whole incident the week before.

But I didn't bat an eye about the piñata.

I had known Dahlia for three months, and it seemed perfectly normal that she would have a blue Smurf piñata in her car. She also had pink wooden Dutch shoes, an empty hamster cage, and a hula-hoop in the backseat.

But the ride home was suspicious. We had Sixth Period on opposite sides of the campus, with my study hall near the exit. Dahlia ran full out across campus to catch me after school.

"How 'bout I take you home?" she huffed and puffed at me.

Like I said, I didn't really want her near Cruz, and I didn't think her enthusiasm for giving me a ride was about me.

"Thanks but it's so pretty out, I'll just walk," I said.

"You can't refuse a ride home."

"I think I'll pass, but thank you."

Dahlia wouldn't take no for an answer. I said "no" nicely in about four different ways, but she just ushered me toward her car, pushing me from behind with one hand.

It was easy to pick out her car in the parking lot. There weren't a whole lot of glittery purple cars, and when she beeped it open, it played La Cucaracha with its horn. She sang along with the music and waved at the other students in the lot, who had turned to see what was making the racket.

"Here we are!" she announced after our short ride, parking in front of my house. "Yes, I would love to come in," she added, even though I didn't ask.

Dahlia was a great friend. She was probably the nicest person I had ever met. Normally I would have been thrilled for her to come to my house and spend time with me, but the thought of having to suffer through her and Cruz flirting or worse made me want to run screaming.

I got out of the car, closing the door behind me. Dahlia walked around, and I was surprised that she was holding the piñata in one hand and a large, round wrapped present in her other hand.

"What the—" I started.

"Don't you know what day it is?" she asked me, smiling.

The front door opened, and Cruz stepped out wearing a cone-shaped party hat. He blew a party favor, making a terrible noise. "Happy birthday!" he shouted.

It was December ninth, my birthday. I was officially seventeen, and I had forgotten all about it. Cruz had remembered, however, and I learned that when he walked Dahlia out to her car last week, he had leaned in and whispered into her ear his plan for a little surprise birthday party.

No kiss.

No flirting.

He had been planning a party for me.

Inside, the dining room was decorated in streamers made out of cut construction paper, taped into colorful links. On the table was a large pizza, a plate of fries, a tub of Haagen Dazs, and a birthday cake with my name on it.

"Did you win the lottery?" I asked Cruz.

"I found some change under the couch cushions," he said.

Total lie. I had already searched for change under every cushion in the house.

"I don't remember the last time I had a birthday party," I said, staring at my cake.

Another total lie. The memory was burned into my brain like a hot poker or mad cow disease. My last party had been two years ago. My mother invited all her friends—and only *her* friends–but she forgot to tell them the party was for my birthday. They got drunk and ate my coconut birthday cake without a candle, a song, or a birthday wish. For the finale, my mom screamed at me around nine to go up to my room because it was an adult party.

I never got the chance to eat my birthday cake, which was a good thing. I'm allergic to coconut.

Cruz had bought me a chocolate cake with chocolate icing. It had red and green flowers and in the middle was written: Happy Birthday, Tess.

It was perfect.

We started with the pizza and fries. I ate three slices, and I noticed Cruz ate four.

"How does it feel to be an old lady?" Dahlia asked me with her mouth full of fries.

"Hey, you're going to be eighteen in April," I said. "That's nearly a year older than me."

"And don't I wear it well?" she said, tucking a French fry behind her ear and posing like a movie star.

"And how about me?" Cruz asked, posing with a slice of pizza on his head.

I looked at my two friends—the only friends I had ever had—who were wearing food and had clearly gone crazy, and I burst out laughing. I laughed so hard I couldn't breathe. I did that thing they do in the movies where they double over and slap their knee, trying to catch their breath. And I snorted. My eyes teared up, and my nose ran. It went on forever. I had never laughed like that in my life. Finally, it died down to some gasping giggles.

"I wonder what she found so funny," Cruz said to Dahlia. He took the slice of pizza off his head and took a big bite.

I burst out laughing, again.

Cruz hung the piñata on the light fixture and let me have the first whack at it. I took a broom handle and let fly. I only needed to hit it three times before the candy rained down on the table.

"Remind me never to make you angry at me," Dahlia said.

"Or never to give her a broom," Cruz said.

We managed to eat the entire pizza and most of the cake and ice cream. Before we cut the cake, they turned out the lights and lit twenty candles: Seventeen for my years. One for good luck.

One to publish a book. One to move to Paris. They sang Happy Birthday in French, and I blew out all the candles in one blow.

"This was the best birthday I've ever had," I said. "Thank you so much."

"Wait! We forgot the presents!" shouted Dahlia. "Open mine first. Open mine first." She hopped up and down and shoved her present at me. I ripped open the paper, and inside was a round box.

"It's a hat!" Dahlia announced and then clapped her hands over her mouth. "Oh, damn. I didn't mean to ruin the surprise, but I got so excited."

I opened the box. Dahlia had gotten me the most beautiful hat I had ever seen. It was a brilliant, royal blue with a wide, floppy brim and giant black bow on the front. It was a movie star hat.

"I saw the hat in your room, and it gave me the idea," Dahlia said. "Try it on. I think you'll look like Emma Stone."

"Emma Stone. Right." I tried it on. I felt glamorous in it, like someone had replaced me with an entirely new and better me. "How do I look?"

"Like Emma Stone!" Dahlia said.

"Beautiful," Cruz said, and I felt my face go burning hot. He handed me his present. "Here," he said. "Open it."

"But—" I started. I couldn't imagine him spending so much money on me. First the party and then a present.

Cruz put his hand on mine. "I got a shoot last week. Three hundred dollars. They paid cash."

"Are you a model?" Dahlia asked him.

He shrugged. "Trying to be."

"I think you'd be good at that," she said. She formed her fingers into a square and looked at him through the center. "Yep. I see potential. Mauve aura. Sort of a Clark Gable chin thing happening. Raw emotional media magnetism. I think you're going to make it."

"Thanks, I think," Cruz said.

I didn't know what Dahlia was talking about. You'd have to be blind not to think Cruz was going to make it as a model. He was the best-looking guy. Ever. In the world. In the universe.

"Open it," he said to me.

I tore the paper but slowly this time. My mind raced with trying to figure out what was in the box. It was too big for Pop Tarts. Ditto for cash. It was the wrong shape for a hat. I glanced over at Cruz. He was way too happy. I was scared.

"Don't be scared," he said. "Open it already. You'll like it."

"I'm not scared," I lied, ripping at the paper. "So totally not scared."

"She's scared," Dahlia said.

"So totally scared," Cruz agreed.

I ripped off the rest of the paper in three swipes and threw off the box's lid, in a show of bravery. I almost shouted "ta da" but I was stopped by the pink tissue paper cradling a red dress inside the box.

"It's a party dress!" Dahlia cried.

"For you to wear to Dahlia's party. I saw the invitation in your room," Cruz explained to me.

I had been worrying about what to wear to Dahlia's family's fancy Christmas party, but I never shared those worries with Cruz. He just knew somehow, and he had gone out and bought me a red dress.

"You don't like it," Cruz said. "I should have gotten the black, but I thought red would go with your complexion."

My complexion? Did I have a complexion? Did red go with my hitherto unknown complexion?

"I love it," I said.

"Take it out of the box," Dahlia whispered in my ear.

"Oh, yeah. I forgot." I slowly pulled the dress out of the box. It was off the shoulder with long sleeves. It had a tight bodice and pouf skirt. It was a princess dress. An Audrey Hepburn dress. Emily Dickinson would have knifed someone to get her hands on a dress like this.

My dress.

"You're not saying anything," Cruz said.

"I forgot how to speak," I said. "I swallowed my tongue. I had an aneurysm."

"She likes it," Dahlia said.

Cruz nodded. "Yeah, I think she does."

"Loves it," Dahlia said. "Try it on, Tess."

Like a model? Was she kidding? I wasn't going to parade around and pose and be *looked* at.

Studied? Scrutinized? Nuh uh.

Besides, there was no way it would fit. The princess Audrey Hepburn dress would never ever, not in a million years, not in parallel universes, not with air brushing or axle grease, fit me.

"It's your size," Cruz said.

"It's going to look great," Dahlia said.

I didn't try it on for them. I stood, held it up, and thanked Cruz. They stopped asking me to model it, and instead we finished eating the cake. The party ended after that. Cruz insisted on cleaning up, and I took my beautiful gifts to my room.

I hung the dress on the back of my door and stared at it for two full days before I worked up the guts to try it on. It fit perfectly, falling to just above my knees in a flouncy swirl of red luxury. Somehow, Cruz picked out the perfect size of the perfect dress for me.

The perfect boy strikes again.

Armed with the perfect dress, I was actually looking forward to the Christmas party. Now that I would be looking the part, I also boned up on current events, reading the New York Times at school. I was prepared to talk all about Russia, and if that grew old, I could fake a conversation about China and our national debt. I was set.

And I was hungry.

The bill situation was getting serious. Cruz got his one modeling job but none since, and whatever secret benefactor he had found to give us rent money had disappeared. We no longer had cable or internet. The pool was a swamp. There was a stack of bills in red envelopes on the kitchen table, and I sold my cell phone and the two TVs. I was tempted to sell my mother's furniture, but something told me she would know—even from far away in Mexico—and skin me alive.

So we were cutting back.

The Pop Tarts were gone and so was the peanut butter. The only meat I had gotten in the past month was the school's Tuesday BBQ sandwich, and I was pretty sure there was no real meat in the school's Tuesday BBQ sandwich.

"If you stand in the center of the kitchen," I said to Cruz. "There's an echo."

"We could give Mother Hubbard some lessons," he agreed.

"There must be something to eat here somewhere," I said

opening the kitchen cabinets. I found a can of beets and an old bulb of garlic that had melted and stuck to the inside of the cabinet. Blech.

Cruz was searching, too. "Holy shit!" he yelled. I jumped and screamed; sure he had found a mouse. "Eureka!"

I squidged my eyes and looked his way. In one hand, he held up an almost empty bag of flour and in the other hand a bag of chocolate chips.

Chocolate. Chips.

Chips made of actual chocolate.

I rubbed my eyes and looked again. The chocolate chips were still there. It was a split the Red Sea kind of miracle.

"I'll borrow a couple eggs from the neighbor," Cruz said and skipped out of the house.

The prospect of warm, homemade chocolate chip cookies was better than winning the lottery. Cruz and I were in a stellar mood. Happy.

When he came back, he measured out the flour, and I measured the brown sugar. We worked as a team, reading each other's mind, knowing what the other needed before they did. Cruz burst out into Ricky Martin songs from the 90s, and I La Vida Loca'd right along with him.

But our shaking Bon-Bons screeched to a halt when we realized we were missing four ingredients, including white sugar.

"Oh," I said, hopping up on the counter, disappointed. I swung my legs, and my stomach growled. Easy come, easy go. I guessed we were going to have canned beets for dinner.

"All is not lost," Cruz said, scooping up a handful of chocolate chips. He wedged himself between my legs and held the chips in front of me. His eyes were fathomless, deeper than the Mariana Trench and a whole lot more beautiful. They drew me in. I fell down, down, down. I wasn't a great swimmer, but it dawned on me that I wouldn't mind drowning in Cruz's eyes.

He took a step closer, until my legs were wrapped around his hips. I gasped. My body grew uncomfortably hot until my insides were melting.

More than melting. Melted. Incinerated. Obliterated. My molecules had broken down to their itty-bitty DNA level and were rearranging themselves into a girl who couldn't speak, move, or breathe.

I got the impression that Cruz's molecules were doing the same thing to him. He had stopped moving, stopped blinking. He focused only on me, on my eyes, watching me for I didn't know what.

"Tess," he said finally. His voice was smooth and low.

Happiness bubbled up in me and popped, forming a big smile on my face. Cruz smiled back and slowly dropped a few chips into my open mouth.

"How's that?" he asked me.

"Rotten," I said, refusing to swallow the chocolate. "What's their expiration date?"

Cruz walked to the other side of the kitchen and examined the bag of chocolate chips. I hopped down off the counter, spit in the sink, and rinsed my mouth under the tap.

"How bad is it?" I asked, drying my mouth.

"Not too bad if we were eating them five years ago."

"Uh oh."

"They're perfect for one thing, though," Cruz said. "You know…" he grabbed another handful of chocolate chips, paused for a second, and hurled them overhand right at me.

"Whoa!" I yelled. "What do you think you're doing?"

"Food fight," he said, smiling.

"You think you have the right to throw food at me?" My voice rose in a screech that could have broken glass. "You stained my t-shirt! How dare you!"

Cruz's mouth dropped, forming a big O. "I'm so sorry, Tess," he said. "I didn't mean to. I just thought that—"

I cut him off. "Cruz."

"Yes?"

"Take that." I scooped a handful of flour and threw it at him. It hit him splat in the face, and I burst out laughing.

"You!" he shouted, pointing at me. "I thought you were really upset."

I grabbed an egg and held it high. "Why did you think that?"

"Uh oh."

I smashed the egg on his chest and smeared it down to his belt. Cruz looked down and smiled.

"The gloves are off," he announced. He grabbed the other egg, and then we were both going at it, smearing each other's bodies with the cookie ingredients and laughing until we and the kitchen were covered in food.

We collapsed against each other, backing up against the fridge. Our laughter died down, as we tried to catch our breath. I rested my head on his chest and listened to his heart pound. He was warm and strong. I knew I shouldn't lean against him like that, but I didn't want to move.

His arms reached around me and pulled me in even further. We stayed locked in an embrace for a while, dripping with goop. Then, Cruz tilted my chin up with two fingers. "You're a big mess, Tess Parker."

It was a fairy tale being locked in Cruz's arms, his face so close to mine, and looking into his brown eyes with so much emotion in them. I felt like the luckiest girl in the universe. Alive. The invisible girl had disappeared into a puff of desire that was growing with every passing second.

"That's not the first time I've been called that," I whisper. "What about you, Cruz Salvaire, you've got flour on your face, chocolate chips in your hair, and egg everywhere."

He wiped a trail of cookie junk off my cheek and flung it on the floor. "You are special," he whispered.

I was wondering if he meant the kind of special who eats paste and wears underpants over her jeans or the kind of special who was—well—special. I didn't have to wonder long for the answer.

In a gentle, swift motion, Cruz touched his lips to mine. My eyes closed, the sensation almost too much to bear. An electrical current traveled the length and breadth of me, starting a humming that got louder and louder, blocking out all other sounds, filling my head until all I could hear was the humming of my own desire. A desire shared by a perfectly beautiful boy who was kissing me in the kitchen by the refrigerator.

His lips were warm and soft, bordered by the rough stubble that grew on his face. I had never felt something so wonderful—soft, rough, soft, rough–and I wondered briefly if all kisses were this good.

At first, Cruz was tentative, gently touching his lips to mine and pulling away then coming back for more. Little kisses. Little tastes, like he was testing the waters. With one arm wrapped around my waist, he slipped the other behind my head and pressed more firmly against my mouth.

My lips opened to him, an invitation from the woman inside me I was yet to become. Our bodies touched, hard sinking into soft. He cocked his head to the side and deepened the kiss even further, his tongue probing my mouth and making me go crazy.

He moaned, or I moaned—I couldn't tell between us any longer. I clutched onto his back, my fingertips digging into his flesh. He moved us away from the refrigerator, never breaking our kiss, and lifted me onto the counter, wedging his body between my legs, grinding hard against my pelvis.

We were moving faster toward an outcome I had never imagined would happen with him. Not now, not ever. But I knew we were going to get there, knew it as sure as I knew anything, and I didn't want to stop it.

Chapter 12

Love is anterior to life, posterior to death, initial of creation, and the exponent of breath.

--Emily Dickinson

Many physicists believe in alternate or parallel universes. In these universes, there are an infinite number of each of us, leading different, sometimes wacky existences. In one universe, I may be made out of bubble gum or shrink-wrap. In another, fire may be cold and ice may be hot. You get the picture. Being kissed and held by Cruz in the kitchen made me a believer in alternate universes.

Before the kiss, I was a scared and sad little girl. Now, on the road towards intimacy with Cruz, I was something totally different. I couldn't put a name on it, because I had never experienced it before. Later I would know what it was—I was in love—but for that moment, the transformative feeling I felt in Cruz's arms was no less miraculous than being made out of bubble gum.

He kissed me with new urgency. I ran my fingers through his hair and pulled him even closer. His hand slipped under my shirt and cupped my breast, and I gasped in surprise and pleasure. "Cruz," I said against his mouth, my voice hoarse and deeper than usual.

Suddenly, he stopped. I sat on the counter with my eyes closed, the humming still loud in my head. But Cruz was gone, his lips nowhere to be found. I opened my eyes, and there he was in front of me. His eyes were wide, his forehead furrowed, his mouth pulled down in a frown. He was the picture of pain. Anguish. He stumbled backwards, his focus shifting from my face to the floor.

"Don't look at me," he commanded.

"What?"

"Don't talk to me!"

"But—"

"Quiet! I have to think." He turned around in a circle, looking down, as if he had dropped something and was searching for it.

"Cruz—"

"I mean it! Don't talk to me!"

I started to cry, tears flowing down my face and throat, making me choke. I sputtered and sniffed. "Did I do something wrong?" I wailed. "I'm so sorry. I'm so sorry. What did I do?"

Cruz turned in a circle again and then punched the refrigerator, pushing it back a foot. "Goddamn it!" he shouted. "Goddamn it!"

I slipped down off the counter. I cried deep, heaving sobs. I wiped my eyes on my sleeve and took a couple steps toward him. I would have done anything for him to hold me again and tell me everything was all right. "Cruz," I started and reached for him.

"Do *not* touch me!"

I flinched backward and hugged myself so I wouldn't break into a million pieces. The humming had stopped and was replaced with a dark, silent void. I had gone from euphoria to despondence in a heartbeat, and I was disoriented from it.

Cruz turned away from me and put his hands on the counter. I could hear his breathing, ragged and coming in short, loud bursts like a locomotive. He was a stranger to me in that moment, if I had ever truly known him before. I didn't know. I didn't know anything.

"This place is a mess," he said after a long time. "If you think I'm cleaning this up, you're crazy."

I shuddered at his tone: Anger. Hate. "You are just as much responsible for this mess as I am," I bawled.

"I am not," he said.

"Yes you are! You're not being fair!"

"Look and what you did to me!" he yelled. "I'm a mess. I'm going to take a shower."

He stomped out of the kitchen and up the stairs without looking back. I stood in the center of the kitchen, not moving for a few minutes, shell shocked and staring in the direction of the other room, expecting him to come back any second and erase what had just happened. But my miracles were used up, and I was returned to my own universe with a brutal dose of reality.

I was no longer made of bubble gum; I was scared and sad once again.

And heartbroken.

Love is glorious beauty made perfect happiness in the arms of another, but it is sharper than a knife and twice as destructive in the wake of its rejection.

I wet a sponge and wiped at the counter, which was covered in flour and eggs. I heard the shower turn on upstairs, and the reminder of Cruz's presence made my tears flow again. I wiped them on my sleeve and focused my determination on making the kitchen clean.

Dahlia was honking her *La Cucaracha* horn outside the house. I grabbed my purse and took one last look in the mirror. The red dress fit me perfectly. It was definitely the prettiest thing I ever had on my body.

I hated it.

It made me sad. And mad. And it made me want to become a nudist so I wouldn't have to wear the dress…you know, if I didn't have to be naked to be a nudist.

If I had had anything else to wear to Dahlia's Christmas party, I would have put it on instead. If I had had a socially acceptable burlap bag to wear, I would have worn that. A barrel. A trash bag. Anything.

Just looking at Cruz's birthday present made the pain from last night come back in a rush that made my head ache and my eyes sting. I was wounded, dizzy with shock. I kept forgetting to breathe. My chest was heavy; my lungs didn't want to make the effort.

I wanted to hide in bed under the covers, not go to a fancy party. If I could just sleep my life away, I figured, the memory of last night would vanish in the recesses of my mind behind my anxiety dreams of my mother murdering me.

So I wasn't exactly in a party mood, but it was too late to back out and I didn't want to let Dahlia down. Besides, I couldn't sleep. So the next best thing was to flee.

Escape.

Hide.

Normally those were all great ways to pretend to heal, even if healing was impossible. Therefore, I wanted to get out of the house. Every inch of it reminded me of Cruz, which reminded me of his rejection, which plunged my heart into a black hole.

And black holes aren't good.

Cruz had sort of vanished from the house, but his stuff was still there. I guessed he didn't want to see me—at least for now–and I was scared to see him so that worked out well. I was afraid of what he would say to me. I was afraid he would say goodbye.

Dahlia La Cucaracha'd again, and I quickly ran down the stairs with my overnight bag. I left a note for Cruz on the kitchen table, reminding him that I would be gone until the next day, even though I wasn't sure if he cared.

"You look so pretty! Like Emma Stone!" Dahlia shouted from her car. I put my bags in the back seat and sat next to her. She was wearing a floor-length, silver gown, low-cut and sleeveless. She was a dead ringer for Ginger Rogers down to her silver shoes. Her hair fell to her shoulders in thick ringlets with a big red bow on the top of her head.

"You look glamorous," I said.

"Good! That's what I was going for." Dahlia flipped through the radio stations, singing a few seconds of each song before changing her mind to go up and down the dial again. "I'm so excited about tonight. I've been waiting to spring your surprise on you."

She burned rubber, speeding away from the curb. I noticed she didn't bother looking for oncoming traffic. I double-checked that my seat belt was snug.

"I thought my surprise was my birthday party and my hat."

"That was Cruz's surprise," she said, still flipping through radio stations and singing bits of various songs. She seemed to forget her train of thought and then hopped right back on it. "My surprise is coming up tonight at the Christmas party," she announced with glee, swerving through traffic and driving twice the speed limit.

"This is going to be the best Christmas party ever," she announced. "I love Christmas. I love Thanksgiving, too. And July

Fourth. And St. Patrick's Day. I love potatoes. Do you love potatoes? I do. Have you had them with Gruyere Cheese? Love Switzerland!"

Dahlia was the most upbeat, positive person I had ever met. She was full of life and loved every minute she was on earth. Nothing and nobody got her down. Despite how miserable I was after the kiss debacle with Cruz last night, I couldn't help but smile, watching Dahlia sing Katy Perry at the top of her lungs and then switch to Garth Brooks a couple seconds later.

I wondered what Dahlia would say about Cruz, the kiss, and the fight. Would she be able to put a positive spin on it? Could she explain why Cruz did what he did? I didn't know how I should feel. I couldn't get beyond the pain of being rejected, the shock of being kissed, and the fear of losing Cruz forever.

But I couldn't bring myself to say anything to Dahlia about it. I couldn't say the words out loud. If I did, it would make Cruz's rejection more real, and it was already too real. I hadn't even written about it. My first kiss. My first real loss. There weren't enough words in the English language to write all that I experienced and how I felt about it.

Last night, I stood in the kitchen, listening to the water from Cruz's shower run through the pipes of the house. I figured he was washing me off of him, scrubbing away his moment of lunacy when he kissed the pathetic invisible girl.

I couldn't stop my tears, so I tried to distract myself with cleaning the kitchen. But wherever I cleaned, the memories came back to me on a visceral level. I wiped off the counter, and I could feel his body between my legs, his lips on mine. Cleaning off the refrigerator, I saw Cruz's rage at kissing me, hitting the fridge with all his strength.

I scrubbed every surface and got down on my hands and knees to wash the floor. By the time I was done, the kitchen shined, and I was exhausted. I stood in the center of the kitchen again and listened. There was no sound from upstairs. Not a peep from Cruz. It was as if I was the only one in the house.

I choked back a tear at the thought that perhaps soon I really would be the only one in the house, alone to fend for myself. I turned off each light and slowly walked up the stairs, pausing and listening at each step for Cruz.

I don't know what I expected. For him to run down and apologize? For him to sweep me up in his arms and tell me it was all a mistake and that he loved me? For him to continue the fight?

It took me forever to climb the stairs. But I arrived at the top, and the house was still quiet. Nothing had changed. I got my robe from my bedroom and went to the bathroom to take a shower.

For the first time in three months, Cruz had hung up his wet towels. They were folded neatly on the towel rack, the ends matching up. Perfect. I touched them--still warm and damp. The whole bathroom smelled of him.

Apples and sunlight.

I stopped in front of the mirror. I was a complete wreck. My hair was stuck to my head in patches and frizzy and wild in others. My clothes and face were covered in cookie ingredients.

There were chocolate chips in my hair.

I leaned closer to the mirror to study the place on my chin rubbed raw by Cruz's stubble. It was the only proof that I had experienced my first kiss. Otherwise, I looked just like him: Pain and anguish as if someone traded my head for someone else's.

I took off my clothes and stood under the shower, letting the hot water run over me while I shed silent tears. I seemed to have a never ending ability to cry, and it lasted longer than the hot water. When I couldn't stand shivering any longer, I got out.

No, I didn't sleep, and I didn't even try. I lay in bed all night; my eyes wide open in my dark room, listening for any sign from Cruz. But there was no sign. I didn't even hear him stirring in his bed in the next room.

No signs.

No answers.

The next morning I heard the front door shut. Cruz had slipped out before six. I checked his room to make sure he hadn't moved out altogether. His stuff was still there, but I knew we would never be the same. So, it was a relief—sort of—to get out of the house, even if I had to risk my life with Dahlia's driving in her small, glittery car.

"I told my father we must have hula dancing at the party, and you know what he said?" Dahlia asked, driving like a bat out of hell to her house.

"Hula dancing?" I asked.

"Exactly! 'Hula dancing?' he asked like he didn't know what it is. Can you imagine?"

Dahlia continued to flip through the radio stations while she turned onto a long driveway lined with tall palm trees and ended at the foot of a mansion.

"Is this the White House?" I asked, sticking my head out the window.

"No, silly. It's yellow."

It was yellow. Lots and lots of yellow. I couldn't imagine how much yellow paint it took to paint Dahlia's ginormous palace. A million gallons of paint. Two million.

A lot of paint.

The mansion was at least three stories high with giant windows and columns just like in *Gone With the Wind*. I looked up at the mansion, and my mouth popped open. I was mildly worried that a seagull would fly by and poop in my mouth, but for the life of me, I couldn't close it. The house was really big.

Dahlia parked her car in front, and a valet jumped around to her door and opened it for her. "How many people live here?" I asked her.

"Just my family."

"How many people are in your family?"

"My dad, my mom, and me," she said, counting on her fingers. That sounded about right. The house was just big enough for her family…and the entire city of San Diego.

The valet skipped around to my side and opened the door. He handed me my bag and parked the car among the Bentleys, Porsches, and Maserati's.

I grabbed Dahlia's shoulder. "Dahlia, what kind of military is your father? Does he *own* the army?"

"He's in the navy. A captain. But my mother's grandfather invented Saran Wrap."

"Wow," I said, looking up at the columns. "I use Saran Wrap!"

The front door was a couple stories high. A man in butler clothes opened it before we even knocked.

"Thank you so much, Martin," Dahlia said and punched his upper arm, playfully.

"I'm with Dahlia," I said because I was more or less sure someone was going to throw me out. I so did not belong there.

Dahlia was Saks Fifth Avenue.

I was Walmart.

Inside, there was marble everywhere and a long circular staircase. The house was decorated from top to bottom for Christmas, and classical music was playing from another room.

"May I, Miss?" the butler asked me and took my bags.

"Take those up to my room, please," Dahlia instructed

him. She tugged me behind her. Her long, silky dress swished along the marble floors as she walked, and I stumbled behind, my mouth still open, trying to take in every bit of luxury and opulence of her house.

We entered a huge living room. A monster fireplace took up most of one wall, and at least ten couches and countless armchairs filled the room. I had seen pictures of Hearst Castle and this was right up there with that.

As big as it was, it was filled with wall-to-wall people, standing and sitting, eating the hors d'oeuvres, which were passed around on silver trays by men in tuxedos, and drinking champagne from crystal flutes. Someone played relaxing classical music on a concert grand piano at the end of the room, along with other musicians, who played a whole selection of violins and cellos.

The guests were impeccably dressed and made up. Ball gowns and tuxedos. Armani and Chanel. These were the beautiful people I had read about, I realized. Rich. Successful. The crème de la crème of society.

I hoped nobody would talk to me.

Dahlia pulled me to the center of the room, spun around and announced as loud as she could, "Ladies and gentlemen, please welcome my best friend! We are going to have such a good time!"

There was no reaction from the partiers. They continued chatting among themselves, and the musicians didn't miss a beat. I thought that nobody noticed us at all. But a tall, imposing man in a dress navy uniform stormed over. He was fighting mad, and I resisted the urge to run away. He grabbed Dahlia by the elbow and pulled her up against the wall. I followed, even though he scared the bejeezus out of me.

"Just what do you think you are doing, young lady?" he demanded from Dahlia.

"It's a celebration, Daddy!" she yelled.

"Shh. You're making a fool out of yourself, as usual. Can't you quiet down?" He hissed between clenched teeth.

A woman in a designer gown approached us, swaying as she walked. "Now Fred," she said, slurring her speech. "This is a party. No harm, no-no-no foul." She smiled and stumbled. He caught her and took her glass of champagne away.

"If you embarrass me again, you're going upstairs. Do you hear me?" he told Dahlia.

"Yes, Daddy," she said, her voice just above a whisper. Her eyes filled up with tears. "This is my friend, Tess."

"Hello, Tess. Keep your friend in line," he told me. "Don't let her loose the dogs into the kitchen like she did last year. And no dancing on tables!"

He dragged the drunk woman away without looking back. Dahlia wiped her eyes with the back of her hand.

"Never mind him," she said to me. "He's just my father. You know how fathers are supposed to be strict. It's play acting. Not real at all."

I didn't know a thing about fathers because I never had

one, but I was pretty sure her father wasn't play acting.

"All right then," she said, clapping her hands together and grabbing a silver tray of hors d'oeuvres from a server. She popped a mushroom cap into her mouth and offered me the tray. Her mood changed from sad to ecstatic in a split second. She was blowing hot and cold like an air conditioner on the fritz. "Time for your surprise," she said, smiling. "Come on. Follow me."

We wound through the crowd from couch to couch until we found the couch that Dahlia seemed to be searching for. An old couple was sitting on it, speaking to another old couple on a couch facing them.

"Surprise!" Dahlia yelled. "Let me introduce you to Madame and Monsieur Berger."

The old woman turned to her and smiled. "Bonjour!" she said.

Chapter 13

They might not need me; but they might. I'll let my head be just in sight; a smile as small as mine might be precisely their necessity.

--Emily Dickinson

Old people smell. You've probably smelled them. They smell like—you know—old. They have a kind of musty scent. Different. Like they've moved on to being not quite who they were. They're people plus.

Evolved.

I love the smell of old. Everything old. People, books, buildings.

There's not a lot of old in San Diego, and there wasn't a lot of old in my life. No grandparents and my mother liked to hang with a younger crowd.

Monsieur and Madame Berger smelled like really old—ancient old—in a cloud of expensive perfume and cologne. I liked them immediately, even though they were different from any people I had ever met.

Madame Berger dripped diamonds. She was covered in shining, shimmering rings, bracelets, necklaces, and earrings. It was like Zales had opened a store on her tiny body. She wore a navy blue Chanel suit, and her hair was perfectly done in a hairsprayed mound on her head.

Monsieur Berger was dressed in slacks, a black turtleneck, and a blue smoking jacket with a coat of arms on his chest pocket. A nobleman. I wondered what he thought about the French revolution. I wondered how his ancestors escaped the guillotine. He took a cigarette out of a gold case and lit it, blowing a thin trail of smoke above him.

This was my first contact with French people. They weren't at all what I had expected. I expected a whole different smell with fewer diamonds.

"Bonjour ma belle," Madame Berger said to Dahlia, who hopped up and down before she gave the old woman two kisses on her cheeks. European style. "So much energy," Madame Berger observed.

She was right. Dahlia plopped onto the couch arm next to Madame Berger. She tapped her feet on the floor, and bounced up and down in place, as if she was riding a horse.

"Madame Berger, this is Tess Parker, the one I told you about."

"Mais oui. Mais oui," Madame Berger said, putting on her glasses in order to study me better. "Come here," she told me in a thick accent.

I took a couple steps toward her and leaned down. "So fresh," Monsieur Berger said. "N'est-ce pas?"

"Yes, so fresh," Madame Berger agreed.

I didn't know what "fresh" meant, but it was obviously good because they were smiling, and they signaled for me to sit next to them on the couch.

Dahlia clapped her hands. "This is great! This is great! It's like the sun and stars aligning, or you know, Twinkies." She jumped up, and skipped across the room, bumping into a server and sending a plate full of bacon-wrapped scallops flying through the air to land on a half dozen of San Diego's elite. Without missing a beat, she skipped off to the next room. I wondered if I should run after her.

"Stay with us," Madame Berger said, reading my mind. Her bony hand clutched onto my arm with surprising strength. "We 'ave only just met."

They explained that they lived part-time in an apartment in Paris and the rest of the time in a house in the south of France, but they were about to go on a cruise around the world for four months. It sounded like heaven, a life I had only dreamed of.

"Where do you summer?" Monsieur Berger asked me.

"The same place where I winter, spring, and fall," I said.

He laughed. "Delightful!" he said. "Such a robust sense of humor."

I didn't have the heart to tell him I wasn't joking.

"Tell us what you want to become in life," Madame Berger requested.

I didn't often tell people I wanted to be a writer. It was almost embarrassing. I was more the dental assistant, office receptionist kind of girl, and telling people I wanted to be Hemingway was sure to bring in the laughs. But I didn't think the Bergers wanted me to be a dental assistant or a receptionist. I was pretty sure they would like me to say I was going to be a writer. So, I did.

"Comme Pierre," Madame Berger said to her husband.

"Excuse me?" I asked.

"She say you are just as our friend, Pierre. He is also a writer." Monsieur Berger signaled to a man standing by the fireplace, and he walked over to us. He was tall and slim, and he wore a black, fitted suit and shiny shoes. His dark hair was cut short and his eyes were a striking blue.

"Blue," I breathed. He was a very handsome older man, probably in his thirties. He walked with complete self-confidence, but not in a stuck up way.

Swagger.

His eyes shifted to me, and his right eyebrow shot up. "Blue?" he asked me. "That's a lovely name." He spoke with a slightly lighter accent than the Bergers, but he oozed French out of every pore.

"No, I mean, that's not my name," I said.

"Zees iz Tess," Madame Berger told him.

"Another writer, Pierre," Monsieur Berger explained.

"Is that so?" He sat on the chair next to the couch and crossed his legs. "Blue, a beautiful, young writer. My favorite genre of writer."

I couldn't speak. I was in way over my head. I was no good at small talk, not that I had any idea what small talk was for rich French people.

"Tell me what iz it that you write?" he asked me.

"Uh—"

"Let me guess," he said. "I sense a deep intellect in your lovely head. Perhaps you have amazing powers of deductive reasoning. So…a mystery writer?"

He had a way of speaking that made me blush up and down my body. He gave me all of his attention, as if the rest of the world was inconsequential or nonexistent.

I shook my head. I still couldn't find words.

"Ah, I see," he said, smiling and raising his eyebrow again. "You want to make this difficult for me. Very good. Very good. Could you be perhaps a romantic? A woman with such a face could only be a romantic. So, you write the romance?"

I didn't know how to answer him. I didn't actually write anything outside of my notebooks, and in them I wrote little stories…my dreams, my desires, my emotions, and my despair. What genre was that? I wished they hadn't told him I was a writer. I didn't want him to find out that I was just a teenage girl who wrote about her boring life in a 99-cent store notebook.

"I see," he said. "La belle est timide. You are shy." He snapped his fingers, and a server came over with a tray of champagne flutes. He took one and handed it to me. Then he took one for himself. "A toast to writers," he said and clinked his glass against mine.

I had never drunk alcohol before, let alone champagne. I had seen how ugly my mother and her friends got when they were drunk, and I never wanted to become like them. But there was something about Pierre that made me do whatever he said without thinking twice.

I took a sip. It was sweet and not sweet at the same time. It was sharp and not sharp at the same time. It was delicious.

"So, this is what we are going to do," Pierre continued. "I will tell you about my writing because I can see that you are humble, and unfortunately, I am not."

"But surely you have heard of Pierre Ollivier," Monsieur Berger said to me. "He is France's greatest living ecrivain."

I hadn't heard of him. I had only read dead French writers, and not much of those.

"Yes," I managed to say. "Of course, I've heard of him. I love your work."

Pierre leaned his head back and roared with laughter. "Zis girl is perfection! She lies with such charm."

"I didn't lie," I lied. I was a terrible liar. I had never learned the art of it. I wasn't used to speaking to people in general, and to bend the truth, I would sputter and turn bright red.

Pierre leaned over and touched my arm. The hair on the back of my neck stood up, and I thought my eyes would bulge out of my head.

"My beautiful young Blue," he called me. "I am touched that you lied to me. Emu. Do you know what this word means? Do you speak French?"

"Emu? A big, Australian bird?"

"Eh? No. I think I will enjoy teaching you French. In any case, I am a boring, stuffy writer. An intellectual. It takes me ten years to write a book."

"Masterpieces," Madame Berger said.

"Masterpieces," Monsieur Berger agreed.

"I would love to read them," I said, this time telling the truth. He was mesmerizing. A real author close up, who was actually talking to me.

"Too bad we do not have more time," he said. "I would love to talk to you about writing. So often, I lack intellectual company."

"Perhaps in June when she come to Paris," Madame Berger said.

I almost dropped my drink. "Excuse me?" I asked.

"You can show her the Sorbonne when you are there," she continued.

"Ah, you are a student in my home?" Pierre asked me.

I didn't know what to say. Had Dahlia told them about my dream to go to the Sorbonne in France? Did she tell them that I wanted to be a writer?

"Well, not exactly. I mean, not yet," I said.

"In June," Madame Berger said. "She is staying in our chambre de bonne for one year. We are delighted to host a writer!"

I didn't exactly pass out. Okay, maybe I did. I mean, I did drop the glass of champagne and sort of melt off the couch and onto the floor, like a cartoon character.

Like I had no bones.

Like a de-boned chicken or a really, really drunk girl with no bones.

No, I had no idea what a chamber de bonne was—I really had to learn French—but I knew what "staying" meant. Ditto "host" and "one year." Could it be true? Could these rich people be hosting me for a full year in Paris?

There's a saying that goes like this: Be careful what you wish for because you might just get it. In my experience, I never got a single thing I wished for. So, I never actually worried about the saying.

So, why did I sort of pass out?

Why did I wind up catatonic, lying under the coffee table with my dress hiked up to my blue polka dotted panties? The answer was simple. I was in shock that something good was going to happen to me.

Shock.

I was dimly aware of the music stopping, and a large group of people surrounding me.

"Is she drunk?" I heard one person say.

"She only had one sip of champagne." I recognized that voice as Pierre's. He was so dreamy. Rich and successful in a beautiful suit and fabulous swagger. And he called me Blue.

Blue. My very first nickname in my whole life.

Everyone around me had a theory about why I passed out. They had a running debate about my health.

"She's in a coma."

"Shut up, Doris. Her eyes are open. You close your eyes if you're in a coma."

"Shut up, Philip. You're an imbecile."

"I've seen this before in Ghana: Typhoid."

I heard gasps and some shifting around, as some of the people obviously decided to stand a safe distance away from a possible Ebola victim.

"I'm a doctor, and I can tell you this is not typhoid."

"What the hell!" I recognized that voice, too. It was Dahlia's father. He had a very commanding, militaristic voice. "Stand back!" he ordered, and the guests all dutifully complied.

He lifted the coffee table off me.

"In France, zis iz what we do," Madame Berger announced and spilled her glass of champagne on my face. I sputtered and coughed and sat up straight.

"I told you it wasn't typhoid," someone said from the crowd. The musicians started playing again, and most of the guests milled about the room, bored with me since I wasn't in a coma and I didn't have a catastrophic disease.

"What happened?" Dahlia's father asked me, helping me to my feet.

"What's a chamber de bonne?" I asked.

"She's talking gibberish," he said and sat me on the couch. "Perhaps she should go upstairs and lie down."

But I didn't want to lie down. I wanted to know all about the good thing that was going to happen to me. I wanted to know every detail to make sure it was real. I asked Madame Berger to explain exactly what she was talking about, and after she did, I asked her to repeat it.

Luckily, Madame Berger didn't get impatient with me.

Instead, she seemed to enjoy my enthusiasm for her offer.

"A small room," she explained. "You know at the very top of our building. How do you say in English? Garret. Clean with ze bathroom down the hall. In a good quartier, of course. Neighborhood, you understand."

I nodded and gulped. "The thing is—" I started. I didn't know how to broach the subject of money. It seemed that they were offering me a gift of a year in an apartment they owned, but what if I was mistaken? What if they wanted to rent me the room for a huge amount of money that I could never possibly come up with?

"I think Blue is worried about the rent, Madame," Pierre said, making me blush. I looked down and picked an invisible piece of lint off my dress.

"Rent?" Madame Berger asked. "No rent. No loyer. Zis iz a gift. We are patrons of the arts. We are your host, ma belle. One year in the chamber de bonne while you study at the Sorbonne and write your fabulous book."

She stuck her finger in the air. One. One year to stay for free in Paris.

Could it be that everything I had always wanted was really going to happen?

"I will give our coordinates to Dahlia. It will be all arranged," Madame Berger said. "Ah, there iz Miss Dahlia."

Dahlia skipped over to us. She was flushed, and there were beads of sweat on her forehead. "They're about to gong the gong. I hope you like lamb," she said to me.

It turned out that I loved lamb. In fact, everything tasted amazing, now that I was the happiest person on the planet. The dining room was as big as our school's gym. The walls were made out of a deep cherry wood, and a long table was laid out in the center. The entire room was lit in candlelight, and a harpist and two violinists played soft music in the corner.

Dahlia and I were seated far away from Pierre and the Bergers. From my seat, I couldn't speak to them anymore about the apartment in Paris, but Dahlia was more than happy to give me more details. In fact, she couldn't seem to stop talking.

"I've been to their place. Huge! A palace right in the heart of the city overlooking the Seine and the Louvre. You know, the museum that used to be the king's crib."

I nodded.

"The maid's room was empty. So, they were thrilled to give it to you, especially when I told them you were the next Gertrude Stein. You know, except prettier of course. More mashed potatoes?"

She scooped potatoes from a server's dish and plopped them onto my plate. She had done that with the lamb, salad, and carrots, too. My plate was piled high, and I was on second helpings. I could never eat that much, and I was kicking myself for not bringing Ziplocs to sneak the leftovers back home. I had enough for a week, if I could figure out a way to get it out of there.

"Oh, look who's here!" she yelled. "Jonathon!"

Dahlia dropped the dish of potatoes back on the table, jumped up, and ran around to the other side of the table. She gave the man a big hug, which was hard to do since he was sitting down, and she wound up elbowing the woman sitting next to him right in her face.

Dahlia's father saw the whole debacle from his seat at the head of the table. He threw his napkin down and stormed over to her. I noticed her mother was still drinking instead of eating. She sort of rocked in place as if she couldn't find her balance in her chair. I became transfixed, not daring to look away because I was sure she was going to fall face first into her dinner.

"Dahlia!" her father shouted and pushed her away from Jonathon and the woman who now had a big shiner. "That's enough," he said. "You two can finish upstairs. I'll have your suppers sent to you."

"But Daddy," Dahlia wailed. "I want to dance!" She pirouetted and kicked the air. Her father shot me a pleading look.

I ran over and wrapped my arm around Dahlia's waist. "Let's have a slumber party," I said in her ear. That seemed to mollify her, and she took my hand and ran gleefully upstairs, tugging me behind her.

Dahlia's room was huge, beautiful, and surprisingly old school. She had a king sized canopy bed, a large wood desk, two couches, and a big armchair. But no electronics. No big screen TV.

Her room was chill. You know, in a richer-than-

Madonna's-daughter kind of way. I loved it. I felt completely relaxed there. Calm. My heartbreak and fears of survival faded away in her bedroom. It was a fortress of Zen. A sanctuary. But not for Dahlia. She couldn't relax or even stop singing. Her eyes were wild, and her body was in a constant state of movement.

"Happy!" she sang while dancing on her desk.

I held up my bag. "Do you mind if I put on my pajamas?"

"Dance with me! Dance with me!"

"I sort of have to pee."

"Pee on the desk!" I didn't think she was totally kidding. She was in some kind of loopy, hyper zone. She was Dahlia times ten with way more energy than I had ever had.

"I would rather pee in the bathroom," I said, feeling like a big party pooper. What did I know about slumber parties? Maybe I was supposed to dance and pee on the desk. Maybe that was the cool thing to do.

Dahlia's father walked into the room, carrying a glass of water in one hand, and a bottle of pills in the other. "The bathroom is over there," he said, pointing to a door. "Feel free to take a long shower. This is going to take a while."

I didn't know what he was talking about, but he was the kind of man who was used to having his orders obeyed. Just before I opened the bathroom door, I turned to see him giving Dahlia two pills. She swallowed them while dancing on her desk.

If Dahlia's bedroom was a sanctuary, her bathroom was nirvana. I never wanted to leave. It was huge and gorgeous and stocked with every beauty product ever invented. If I were Dahlia, I would be the world's cleanest person.

The only problem was choosing between her sunken bathtub and her four shower-headed shower. They both had pros and absolutely no cons. But something in me knew I would never leave the bathtub, and Dahlia might someday really need to pee in an actual toilet instead of on her desk. So, I went for the shower.

I turned it on and let the water hit me from every direction. They say money can't buy happiness, but those people never took a shower in Dahlia's super luxury bathroom.

As I soaped myself up with her aromatherapy beauty bar, the events of the evening replayed in my head like an announcer giving the rundown at the beginning of a television show.

"Last time on Tess Parker's life, we saw Tess fighting with the boy of her dreams," the announcer in my brain said, as I shampooed my hair. "Despondent, she went to her best friend's party and met a famous handsome author and a filthy rich French couple, who gave her an apartment in Paris for an entire year. Even though she refused to pee on her friend's desk, she was looking forward to dessert and using her friend's thick towels to dry off. But questions remain: Would Tess make up with Cruz? Would she survive in her house without money for the next six months? Would she be able to buy a ticket to Paris and get into the Sorbonne? And what were the pills that her friend's father gave her?

Stay tuned for another episode of Tess Parker's Life."

Reluctantly I turned off the shower. I combed my hair and used Dahlia's face cream and perfume. When I left the bathroom, she had stopped dancing and singing and was wrapped in a blanket, lying on a couch in front of the roaring fire in her fireplace.

"All better?" she asked me. She had calmed down, finally—I guessed—tired from the party, the dancing, and the late hour. There was a platter of desserts and hot chocolate on the coffee table in front of her. I sat on the floor with my legs crossed under the table.

"Yes," I said. "Thank you. That was the best shower ever."

"Let's have cake."

We each chose a slice of cake and took a bite. It was chocolate and raspberry. Delicious. We chewed in silence for a long time, staring into the fire.

"Dahlia, I want to thank you for all you've done. You saved my life. You made my dreams come true."

"Shh," she said, touching my shoulder. "Let's just enjoy the dessert and the fire. No need to thank me. It took no effort on my part. Besides, at least one of us should have their dreams come true."

Chapter 14

A wounded deer leaps the highest.

--Emily Dickinson

It took me forever to fall asleep. The minute I actually had good news to share, I couldn't share it with the one person I wanted to share it with. Just a couple of days ago, Cruz would have loved to hear about Paris and Madame and Monsieur Berger. Now, I wasn't sure he ever wanted to see me again.

Good news was like a tree falling in the woods. If nobody was there to hear it, did it make a sound? And was it really good news?

I was trying hard not to think about Cruz. I tried to be happy about Paris instead, but my emotions couldn't get around the sad. It was too big. I had the heartbreak that only people who have never been loved suffer. I had come so close to being loved by Cruz. It had been in my grasp. One kiss that transported me high and then rejection that sent me crashing against the rocks.

If I thought about it, my chest would get heavy, and it became difficult to breathe. So, I stayed up and watched the fire, even when Dahlia fell into a deep sleep on the couch after she finished her piece of cake.

She was a great friend, even if she said it wasn't a big deal to set me up with a free place to stay in Paris. To me, it was the biggest deal. Dahlia had never asked where my mother was, why I was living with Cruz, why I had no money or friends. But she saw my need and found a solution. She was going to communicate with Madame Berger and organize everything for me. I could never thank her enough.

After the fire grew dim, I covered her with another blanket, turned out the lights, and slipped into her bed. When I finally fell asleep, I didn't dream about Paris. Instead, I dreamed about Cruz, his lips touching mine, his arms around my body, pulling me close.

"There's something I need to tell you," he whispered in my dream.

"What?"

He moved his mouth, but no sound came out. "What?" I asked again. "I can't hear you." He kept talking, but I couldn't hear a word. I was certain it was important for me to know what he was telling me, but I couldn't make it out. "Speak louder!" I yelled. "Speak louder!"

I woke up to screams. At first, I thought I was the one screaming through my dreams, but it turned out the sound was coming from outside Dahlia's room, down the hallway.

"Dahlia?" I whispered. I got out of bed. The couch was empty. She was nowhere to be found. A light came through the bedroom's open door.

"Take it easy," I heard a man say. "I'm not going to hurt you."

Then, there were more screams. Dread washed over me as I realized Dahlia was the one screaming. I ran out into the hallway. She was standing at one end in her party dress, her hair in tangles like a rat's nest. She was barefoot, and she was standing like a quarterback, ready to take on the defensive line. Her father was behind her, and in front of her were two men in paramedic uniforms.

I heard sirens in the distance coming closer, and I wondered if that was backup arriving. Dahlia was wild, her eyes spinning in their sockets.

"I'm just trying to finish the song!" she screamed. "I have to finish the song! Get out of my way! Why don't you understand?"

"You can finish the song after you come with us," one of the paramedics told her.

"No!" she screeched. "I have to do it now. I have to go to the roof and do it because the stars are going to help me. Don't you understand? The stars will help me finish the song!"

She wiped at her face with her hand, smearing her makeup. She looked like a wounded, wild animal. Transformed. Unrecognizable. Dahlia had disappeared and a crazed beast had taken her place.

She broke my heart.

I heard heavy boots race up the stairway and two policemen appeared. They quickly assessed the situation, looking from Dahlia to the paramedics to me to her father and back to Dahlia. "You got this?" one of them asked the paramedics.

"We might need some assistance," a paramedic answered.

I got a lump in my throat. I didn't know what was happening, but I did know it was out of my control. Dahlia needed help that I couldn't give her.

"I have to finish my song!" Dahlia screamed. She rocked on her heels and then took off, right at the paramedics.

Red rover, red rover, send Dahlia right over, I thought, watching her try to break through the two men. They caught her with a loud, collective grunt, almost falling over but managing to subdue her.

"Don't hurt her!" I yelled, watching them push her to the floor.

"Don't get involved," one of the cops ordered me. He was all business, and I stepped back and bit my lower lip. The policemen took over, holding Dahlia down while the paramedics dug through their supply of drugs. They injected her with something, and she calmed down immediately. It went quickly after that. A stretcher appeared; they took her downstairs, put her in an ambulance, and took her away just as the sun came up.

Her father and I watched from the driveway as the ambulance and the police car drove away. We stood in the cold morning air in our pajamas and bare feet long after they were gone, watching the empty driveway for what I didn't know. Perhaps we were just trying to digest what we had witnessed or convince ourselves that it actually happened. It was the kind of event that didn't seem real, like a kiss from a perfect boy that was quickly rejected. My first best friend disappeared in a cloud of crazy in the back of an ambulance. How could I ever accept that as being real?

The fresh air and the quiet helped me in that moment of loss, but I couldn't quite stop crying. "Get dressed, and I'll drive you home," Dahlia's father said, finally and walked back into the house. He was stone. Emotionless. But I was a basket case. Nothing in my life had prepared me for what I had just witnessed.

I packed my bag and met him back downstairs after about ten minutes. "Come on," he said and walked me to his Jaguar. He opened the passenger door for me. He started the engine and turned off the radio. We drove for a few blocks in silence.

"This is not the first time, you know," he said. "Or don't you know?"

"Is Dahlia going to be okay?"

"She'll be in treatment for a while. A few months."

"A few months?"

"I knew it was a mistake to send her to school," he said, but I thought he was talking more to himself than to me. "She does better with a tutor. It's probably my fault with all the moves."

"What's wrong with her?"

"Dahlia's bi-polar, been that way for several years."

I gave him directions to my house. He parked in front, got out, and opened my door for me. "It was nice meeting you," he said. "Sorry it didn't work out."

So much didn't work out. My life. My friendship. And now with Dahlia gone, my apartment in Paris hadn't worked out.

He got back into the car and drove off without another word.

I stayed on the sidewalk and watched him go. I had been watching a lot of people leave me, lately, I realized. My mother, Cruz, Dahlia. Alone feels different to every person, but my alone was cold and heavy and made it hard to breathe. That's why my heart did a little leap when I noticed Cruz's car in the driveway. I had feared that he had left me for good, but he was here at least for now.

It was still very early so I was as quiet as possible when I opened the door and walked upstairs. I had a terrible urge to peek into Cruz's room and to tell him about Paris and how I almost had an apartment for a year, about Dahlia and her break with sanity and her trip to parts unknown. But then I remembered the last time I saw Cruz, our horrible fight, and his rejection.

My heart had been broken on so many levels, I wasn't sure it could ever be whole again. But he was there, I wasn't alone, and that made it bearable.

Here's what I figure: If God meant for a woman to have triplets, he would have given her six arms. Mrs. Maclaren and I had had four combined arms, which were two short for handling her toddlers. It had been a crazy day helping her with her kids. One was pooping out of his diaper and eating it—Can you say gross?—while another one was heading for the electrical outlet behind the TV with a fork in his hand. Meanwhile, the third one was just crying because that's how babies are.

Annoying.

I definitely earned my money, and since the Maclaren triplets were being even more gross than usual, their mother paid me extra to sit with them at the end of the evening while she took a bath.

"I owe you so much," she said to me, as she closed the bathroom door.

I was happy to work, happy to be busy and to have my mind off Dahlia and Cruz.

It had been the first day back at school since the Christmas party, and there was no sign of Dahlia. I shouldn't have expected her to be at school since her father had explained that she would be getting treated for months. But I was hoping she would be there, anyway.

Gone was Dahlia. Gone was my only friend at school. And gone was the glamour.

Without her, I went back to being Mess Parker, and school dragged on in tedium, isolation, and fear. I spent the day either watching the classroom clocks move at a snail's pace or reliving the fight with Cruz and Dahlia's breakdown.

Pooping and puking toddlers were a great relief from all

that.

And Mrs. Maclaren fed me, which was good since we didn't have any food in the house.

"Here's what I owe you and something extra," she said handing me five, twenty-dollar bills at ten o'clock that night. "You're my angel of mercy."

What would Mrs. Maclaren think if she knew her angel of mercy had been abandoned by her mother and was saving her money to buy peanut butter?

Thankfully, I was exhausted. I could just shower, go to bed, and not think any more about Cruz or Dahlia. Hopefully, I would be too tired to dream because my dreams had been all nightmares lately and I was waking up more tired than when I went to bed.

When I got home, there were a couple cars parked in front, and Cruz's car was in the driveway. Inside, models were setting up for a party, putting out bottles of wine and rolling joints. I spotted Cruz walking from the kitchen to the living room, and my heart skipped a beat.

I hadn't seen him since our kiss and our fight. He was still the most beautiful boy I had ever seen. He literally took my breath away, and I had to remind myself to breathe or I would pass out. I stared at him, willing him to see me and apologize, but he was busy with his friends and didn't seem to notice me. Besides, I didn't want him to notice me. What if he looked at me with hatred? What if he wasn't the same Cruz anymore?

The doorbell rang and Cruz turned toward it. I ran up the stairs, too chicken to stay in his path. It was a hard position to be in: the rejected invisible girl alone and the beautiful boy downstairs with his perfect, model friends.

The bathroom was clean. No wet towels on the floor. I locked the door and turned on the shower. They must have turned on the music, because I could hear the boom boom of the bass from inside the bathroom. Loud. I finished the shower and went to bed, closing the door behind me. I put my pillow over my head and wished for sleep, but the boom boom bass kept me up.

Also, the loud giggling of the skinny model girls was coming right through my door.

You know that moment when your sad turns to mad?

My sad turned to mad at eleven on that Monday night. And I wasn't just mad, I was fighting mad. I was Khaleesi-somebody-stole-my-dragons mad.

I punched my pillow, got out of bed, opened my door, and stood at the top of the stairs.

"Shut up!" I screamed as loud as I could. "Shut up! Shut up! Shut up!"

But the giggling didn't stop, and the music kept booming.

"Shut the fuck up!" I yelled. "I hate you! I hate all of you! You're all a bunch of fuckers! I hate you! Go to hell! Leave my house!"

I was getting hoarse from screaming, but I wasn't getting

anywhere except more and more upset.

"Shut up!" I yelled again, and then I heard him run up the stairs, taking two steps at a time. I stopped screaming. I stopped breathing.

"What's wrong?" Cruz asked, reaching me at the top.

He was there, face to face with me. I don't know why it came as a surprise. Did I think he wouldn't come up and see why I was screaming like a madwoman? No, I didn't. I thought he would just turn the music down and end the party. You know, ignore me.

But he was there in the hallway with me, his body inches away from mine, concern and anger on his face, and I broke down completely.

"Why are you doing this!" I screamed at him.

"Doing what?"

"You're making all this noise, and I need to sleep." I was crying so hard that my words were coming out slurred. My nose ran, and I wiped it on my sleeve. "Why are you doing this!"

"Calm down. Stop screaming."

"No!"

"I said, calm down."

"No!"

I was crying and screaming at the same time. I was madder than hell.

"I said, shut up!" I screamed. "Tell your whore girlfriends and your loser model friends to go away. I'm trying to sleep! I'm trying to survive!" Cruz's face turned from concern to shock. He clutched my shoulders and gave me a shake. I didn't care. I refused to calm down for him.

That's when I kneed him right in the balls.

Chapter 15

After great pain, a formal feeling comes. The nerves sit ceremonious, like tombs.

--Emily Dickinson

Cruz didn't flinch, and if I didn't manage to give him physical pain, he was emotionally distraught.

"Tess, don't do this. Don't hurt me."

"I hate you!" I screamed and cried even more because I didn't really hate him.

He hugged me hard, pulling the whole of my body against him. I cried deep, wrenching sobs, and he didn't let go. The party was still going on downstairs, but we had slipped back into our own world.

After a long time, fatigue took over, and my crying stopped. "I didn't want any of this to happen," he said, never letting me go. He rested his chin on my head. "You're everything. You're so much better than me. Don't you see that?"

"That's not true," I said.

"Yes it is. You're going to be great. You're going to be a writer, and you're going to live in Paris, and I will always be nothing and nobody."

"Don't say that. That's not true. You're amazing."

Cruz laughed. "No, Tess. *You're* amazing. And you're going to have a great life and meet a great guy."

"You're a great guy."

"No, I refuse to be the one who held you back. Now, you go to bed, and I'll get rid of everyone."

He picked me up in his arms and carried me to my bed. He covered me with my blanket and kissed me lightly on my forehead.

"It will only take a second," he said.

I heard him jog down the stairs, and the music stopped. I heard his voice and then a communal "aww" from the group before the door opened and then much later, closed.

Then, silence.

He jogged back upstairs, and the lights flicked off in the hallway. "Move over," he said in the dark of my bedroom and slipped under the covers next to me, gathering me to him, like two spoons.

"I'm sorry," he said.

"I'm sorry," I said.

"I made you hurt me, and that was unforgivable of me. I'll never play that game again, no matter the pain."

I didn't understand him. Nothing he said made sense to me. But I did know he was warm and comforting and for the first time in days, I felt safe. I fell asleep within minutes and finally slept the dreamless sleep I had been hoping for.

There was only one more day of school before winter break. I had almost made it through a semester at school without anyone catching on that my mother had abandoned me, and I was feeling pretty good.

That is, until I woke up that Thursday morning with a hundred and three temperature, chills, and a monster sore throat.

"You can't go to school," Cruz said, reading the thermometer.

"Take it, again. I'm never sick. It has to be wrong."

"I've taken it three times," he said. "You're sick, like really sick. You have the flu."

I felt horrible. I felt like lions had attacked me and left me for dead and then a truck ran me over.

"I feel fine," I lied. "If you could pass me my jeans, I'll go to school."

I had to go to school. If I didn't, they would call my mother to see why I was absent, and when they couldn't reach her that would lead to all kinds of problems.

"I'll get the Advil," Cruz said and handed me my jeans.

I was going to need more than Advil. I was going to need IV antibiotics, a heart transplant, and chicken soup.

But I took the Advil and pulled my hair into a ponytail without brushing it first. "How do I look?" I asked Cruz.

"Like you have the flu."

He drove me to school and insisted on picking me up afterward. I didn't argue. There was no way I could walk home. In fact, I didn't think I would make it past third period.

But I did make it through the day. I fell asleep in math class, but otherwise it went by without a hitch. I had an appointment with Mrs. Landes, the college advisor, during the last period, to update me on the Sorbonne, which kind of perked me up.

"France works differently," she told me. "I've been doing my research. They have a different admissions process. They've never even heard of the SATs. And it looks like with your grades, you're a shoe in for the Sorbonne."

"Shoe in is good, right?"

"Yes, in old people speak, 'shoe in' means good."

I would have cried, but my fever had burned away my last tears. Still, I was happy.

"And there's more," Mrs. Landes said.

"Shoe in more?"

"Good more," she said. "A possibility of a scholarship for tuition and a stipend for living expenses."

I gasped, taking in a whole lot of air.

"A scholarship?" I asked. "I want a scholarship."

"I thought so," she said. "Here's the application for that and for a student visa. If you get it back to me by April first, signed by your parents, I think you have a decent shot. Happy?"

She smiled, and I tried to smile back. I didn't have a shot. I was shotless. There was no way I could get my mother to sign anything by April first.

"Thank you for all your help," I said.

"You don't look particularly happy, Tess."

"Just a little under the weather."

I took the forms and slipped them into my backpack. "Merry Christmas," I said and left her office.

Cruz was waiting for me in his car at the curb. He had left the car running, which was wise, considering the hit or miss aspect of the engine starting. He hopped out when he saw me, took my backpack and helped me into the car.

"I did it," I said. "How do I look?"

"Like you have the flu and you forgot to brush your hair."

"Everyone's a critic."

Back at home, I put on my pajamas, and Cruz tucked me into bed. He surprised me with a can of chicken noodle soup, which he heated up in the microwave. I took more Advil and sipped the soup.

"Now you can rest for two weeks," Cruz said. He sat at the edge of my bed and studied me as if I was going to die any second.

"I'm feeling better," I assured him. "You know what I want to do for Christmas?"

"Nothing?"

"Nothing," I agreed.

We were tired. Surviving took up a lot of energy. I just wanted to sleep for two weeks. Cruz and I had put our fight aside and our kiss too, it seemed. We were good friends again, but there was a tangible tension between us, which we didn't dare comment on.

"I have after Christmas sales to work, but besides that, I want to do nothing," he said.

We had a lot of nothing at home. Without television or the internet, there wasn't a lot to do in the house. "Mrs. Maclaren did give me six movie passes for Christmas, though," I said.

Cruz's eyes got big. "Movie marathon," he breathed.

I fell asleep at four and didn't wake up until ten the next morning. My fever was gone, and so was my sore throat, but I still felt like roadkill.

It was Christmas Eve, and true to our word, we did

nothing. We sat on the couch downstairs with pizza and pretzels, and read to each other. I read Emily Dickinson poetry to Cruz, and he read Car & Driver Magazine to me. The next day we exchanged Christmas presents. Cruz gave me a jar of peanut butter, and I gave him an air freshener for his car. We went to the movies and sat through three films in a row. It was probably the happiest Christmas of my life.

The next day, Cruz was working all day, and that's why I was alone in the house when the doorbell rang. I froze. The doorbell could represent so much bad news: A visit from the landlord to evict us. The water getting shutoff. Ditto the electricity. Or it could be the cops coming to take me away to a foster family.

I tiptoed to the door and peeked through the peephole.

I opened the door. "Martin?" I asked. I hadn't seen him since he let me into Dahlia's house and took my bags to her room. He was still dressed like a butler, but I couldn't imagine what he was doing at my house instead of Dahlia's.

"Miss Tess, Captain Sherman sends you this note." He handed me an envelope.

"Thanks."

"And he requires an answer before I leave."

It dawned on me that I didn't have a phone and no way to be reached except face to face. I was worried about what was in the envelope. I doubted it could be good news, especially considering what was happening the last time I saw him. Still, I did want to know how Dahlia was doing, and I had no way of finding out.

"You probably should open it," Martin said.

I ripped it open. It was typed on Dahlia's father's personal stationery, telling me that Dahlia insisted on seeing me, even though she was not supposed to have visitors at this time of her treatment. He wanted to know if I'd visit her tomorrow at four in the afternoon.

"Of course," I told Martin. "I really want to see her."

He nodded and handed me a piece of paper. "Here's the address. Don't bring any gifts. They won't let her have anything."

I took the bus to Neiman Marcus because Cruz was going to drive me from there to visit Dahlia. The mall was packed with shoppers taking advantage of the after Christmas sales. I was one of the few people not weighted down with shopping bags.

I paused at the door to Neiman Marcus. I really didn't want to spend any time in snooty central, but I was supposed to meet Cruz inside. Why didn't I tell him to meet me at Wetzel's Pretzels? I fit in much more at Wetzel's Pretzels than at Neiman Marcus and besides, they gave free samples.

I could have really gone for a cinnamon sugar pretzel.

I gathered my courage and opened the door. The store was still the same except for the snooty gold Christmas decorations. I ducked and weaved my way to men's cologne, doing my best to avoid the snooty Mcsnootster salesladies, but I wasn't exactly inconspicuous.

I wasn't wearing a designer cocktail dress, hooker heels, and fake boobs like the rest of Neiman Marcus's clientele. Instead, I was wearing Levis, a man's white t-shirt, and the over-the-top hat that Dahlia had given me for my birthday. I figured she wouldn't be too happy to be locked up in a hospital, but the hat might cheer her up.

I found Cruz behind the counter, surrounded by a group of women with artificial looking faces, asking him to spray himself with the different colognes so that they could smell his body. They were obviously flirting with him, trying to get his attention, as if he would go out with ancient married ladies.

Would he go out with ancient married ladies?

I wasn't sure. Desperate people can do a lot of crazy things, and Cruz and I could definitely be categorized as desperate.

But I mean, gross.

Gross.

I waved my hand in the air to get his attention, but he was too busy spraying himself and getting sniffed by the rich old ladies to notice me. So I had no choice. I had to actually go up to the counter and drag him out of there. It was exactly what I didn't want to do.

He didn't recognize me at first because of the hat. "Dahling," I drawled, elbowing the ladies aside and putting my hands on the counter. "We are late for our rendezvous." I winked, and I could tell he was fighting off a smile. It was almost fun.

"Yes, of course," he said. "Sorry ladies. I'm done for the day."

"Can we afford a cinnamon sugar pretzel?" I asked him as we walked out.

"No, but let's get one, anyway."

I didn't think the car would ever start. Cruz pulled and pushed the choke and checked under the hood, but it took a good ten minutes of the car wheezing and coughing before it finally started.

"That was a close one," Cruz said.

It was a forty-minute drive to The Lavender Serenity Center, which turned out to be neither lavender nor serene. It was located in Rancho Santa Fe, one of the richest areas in San Diego. Most of the houses there were giant, sprawling estates on acres of land with horses.

From the outside, The Lavender Serenity Center fit right into the neighborhood. A long, winding driveway cut through the property, bordered by a white picket fence. Horses ran free among the eucalyptus trees, and the building itself looked more like a high-end ranch than a center for mentally ill teenagers.

Inside was totally different. Sure, there was a waiting room that looked like a five star hotel lobby, but beyond that, it was like a hospital on Riker's Island.

A bodybuilder orderly buzzed us through the door and a nurse was waiting for us on the other side. "Come this way," she said, ushering us to a small room. "Empty your pockets and put your purse in here," she said, throwing a bin on the table.

"Excuse me?" Cruz asked.

"Some of the guests could hurt themselves with certain items. We're just trying to safeguard their health."

Guests. I wondered if Dahlia thought of herself as a guest.

The nurse walked us to room three-fifteen. At first, I thought she had taken us to the wrong room. Inside, a girl was sitting in a chair, and she looked nothing like Dahlia.

"It's Dahlia," Cruz said to me, reading my mind.

I took a step closer to her. She was wearing pink pajamas and fluffy slippers, and she was half-covered with a thin blanket. Her hair had flattened, just like her personality. Drained of color, she was biting her lower lip and looking down at the floor. She had deflated like a balloon. In the place of her bubbly personality, she was left almost catatonic.

I kneeled down in front of her and put my hands on her knees. "Dahlia?"

She blinked and looked at me, seeming to recognize me for the first time. "You're wearing the hat," she said. A tear rolled down her cheek.

"Of course I wore it," I said. "It's fabulous. I'm Emma Stone in this hat."

Dahlia smiled. "Emma Stone."

"Cruz came, too," I said.

He waved. "Hi, Dahlia."

"Chino," she said. "I'm sorry I didn't dress for the occasion."

"You look great," he said. "I wish I wore pajamas, too."

"I think it's going to be pajamas for the next year." Her tears flowed down her face, and her nose ran. I took the Kleenex box off her bedside table and passed her a couple.

"This is upsetting her," the nurse said. "I think you should leave."

"Go to hell," Dahlia told her.

"Yeah, I think she's done here. She's not supposed to have guests, anyway." The nurse grabbed my arm, and I shrugged her away.

"I'm not done," I said, getting angry. I wanted to defend Dahlia in any way I could, and right then, the only thing I could do was take it out on the nurse.

"Yes, you are," the nurse said. "Come on, or I'll call the orderly."

"Please give us five minutes," Cruz said, putting his hand gently on the nurse's shoulder and diffusing the tension immediately.

The nurse blushed and flipped her hair. Cruz had that effect on women. He was the lady whisperer. She was totally in his spell.

"Well, five minutes can't hurt," she said, smiling. "I'll be right back."

She batted her eyes at Cruz, flipped her hair again, and left the room, bouncing on her heels as she walked. Take it from me, men make women go crazy.

"She's such a bitch," Dahlia said.

"Are they treating you all right?" I asked her.

"I guess so. Practice makes perfect."

I didn't know how much to ask her. I didn't want to pry, but I didn't actually know what was wrong with her, why she was in the hospital, and what she meant by 'practice makes perfect.'

"Come closer," she told me. I kneeled down again, and she leaned forward and whispered in my ear. "When you go to Paris, write to me. Don't forget me, and I'll write to you, too. You're going to have such a wonderful life."

"I'll see you before then," I said. I wasn't even sure I was going to go. I couldn't get a scholarship or a student visa without my mother filling out the paperwork, and it looked like the offer of an apartment had vanished like Dahlia's freedom.

"I don't want you to come here again," she said. "I needed to see you one last time. I didn't want you to remember me like—well, you know."

"It wasn't a big deal." Actually, I would have preferred to

remember her how she was at her house, wild and untamed, instead of here, half-dead and soulless. "I'll visit you every week. At least once a week."

"No. This is the last time. I mean it, Tess. Don't come back here but promise me you'll write when you're in Paris. Promise me." She squeezed my hand, and I squeezed back.

"I promise, Dahlia. I'll write you."

She let go and leaned back. She smiled and closed her eyes.

"You're going to love Paris. You're going to be Hemingway and Fitzgerald," she muttered, closing her eyes. She drifted off. Her head flopped to the side and she fell fast asleep. I covered her with the blanket, and Cruz and I walked out of the room.

Dahlia's father was waiting for me in the hallway. He was in his navy uniform, an imposing figure with ramrod straight posture and a permanent scowl on his face.

"I'd like to speak to you, alone for a moment," he said to me, shooting a quick glance at Cruz.

"I'll wait for you out front," Cruz told me.

"Thank you for coming," Dahlia's father said after Cruz left. "It calmed her down. Being bi-polar is a challenge. She had a distinctly intense manic episode, which you witnessed."

I had heard of bi-polar, but I didn't understand it or what a manic episode really meant.

"But she can be cured, right?"

"She has a long road to travel, but this is a good facility. She'll always have to take medication, of course."

That didn't sound so bad, but something told me it wouldn't be quite that simple.

"That's beside the point," he said, growing even more serious. "I'm about to ship out for six months, and you and I have some unfinished business."

Chapter 16

The possible's slow fuse is lit by the imagination.

--Emily Dickinson

Dahlia's father towered over me. He was an imposing figure. Scary. I couldn't imagine what unfinished business he would have with me.

"We do?" I asked.

"Yes. Dahlia made you a promise, and I intend to keep it."

"You do?"

"She was supposed to organize your housing in Paris for a year, correct?"

I swallowed. Tears stung the back of my eyes. I had lost hope of getting the apartment.

"Madame and Monsieur Berger said they would sponsor me," I said, softly.

"That's my understanding as well. I've spoken to them and have finalized the details. It's set for June first. I know you have school until June fifteenth, but it will be ready and waiting for you whenever you get there. Here's their contact information. Let them know when you have an arrival date. They're good people. A little eccentric, though. But you don't seem to mind that."

He handed me a card with the Berger's contact information. "Good luck," he said, dismissing me now that the message was relayed and he had nothing more to say to me.

I stared at the card for a while, not believing my good luck. An apartment would be waiting for me in Paris on June first. It was an impossible dream come true. I felt like I had fallen through a wormhole into another dimension where dreams came true and good things happened to me.

"Thank you," I croaked.

Then, even though the nurse had banished me and Dahlia told me not to return, I ran back into Dahlia's room and threw my arms around her. "Thank you, my very best friend. You saved my life," I said.

I couldn't stop crying. After I said goodbye one last time to Dahlia, I got my purse and ran past Cruz in the lobby, out the door, and into the parking lot. He chased after me and caught up as I reached the car.

"What is it?" he asked. "Are you okay?"

Was I okay? Why was I crying? How could I explain it to him? How could he ever understand what I was feeling, overwhelmed with so many emotions: disbelief that I was able to go to Paris, trauma of seeing my friend in the hospital, anxiety that I could make my dreams come true, and joy that anything was possible. My senses were bursting, and I didn't know how to handle them.

"Tess? What is it?"

"I think I'm going to Paris," I said, finally.

"So why are you crying?"

"I don't know!"

Cruz started to chuckle, softly at first and then much louder, until he was clutching his side, rolling with laughter.

"Don't laugh at me!" I shouted, slapping his arm. But his glee was contagious, and soon I was roaring with laughter, too.

Cruz drove us to Jack in the Box to eat fifty-cent tacos and talk about Paris. We sat at a table for two by the window, and I told him all about Madame and Monsieur Berger and their offer for the small chambre de bonne in a good neighborhood in the center of Paris.

"This is awesome," he said. "A whole year, rent free. It's like a miracle."

It was. Cruz was so happy for me that I didn't want to tell him about the scholarship, the student visa, and the impossible paperwork that I could never get my mother to sign. But he saw through me and knew somehow that my path to Paris wasn't quite so smooth.

"We'll figure something out," he said after I told him.

"She needs to go to the embassy and sign it there. I have a passport, but I need a visa."

"We'll figure something out," he repeated. I had gotten so far, applying to the Sorbonne and securing an apartment for an entire year, but finding my mother and getting her to do what needed to be done would be slightly more difficult than splitting an atom with a hardware store hammer.

Despite the odds stacked against me, for that moment while eating cheap tacos with Cruz, "we'll figure something out," was good enough.

"Tell me what you're going to do when you get there," Cruz said. "Tell me about what you're going to see."

I did. I laid out every fantasy I ever had about living in Paris, about taking my notebook to a café in the early mornings and writing while sipping a café au lait and eating a buttery croissant, about walking along the Seine as the sun set, about spending hours in the museums, soaking up the art.

"I can picture you there," Cruz said. "I can picture you doing all of those things."

Cruz believed in me and believed that I would make it to Paris and become a great writer. He believed what I had only hoped for. But his belief was catchy, and suddenly I could picture myself in Paris, too, and really believe that we would figure out how to make it happen.

We.

"How much money will you need?" he asked me.

"As much as I can get."

"You don't have any hidden away, by any chance?"

"No. I had some, but—" I bit my lower lip. "Well, the thing is—"

Here's the thing about having a rotten mom. You can know you have a rotten mom. You can even tell someone you have a rotten mom. But you always hold out a kernel of hope that you're wrong, that she's going to come back into your life and *poof* transform into a cookie-baking, hugging supermom. And if I said out loud just how rotten she really was, how she stole all my money, it would make it real, and I couldn't hope that I was wrong any longer.

But here's the other thing. Cruz deserved my honesty. Cruz deserved my everything.

I told him about my summer's savings and the empty cookie tin. He listened to my story without interrupting, and when I was done, he put his hand on mine and said, "We'll figure something out."

We ate ten tacos and drank a gallon of Diet Coke. It had gotten late, but we couldn't stop talking. Cruz told me funny stories about his work at Neiman Marcus, about the woman who was allergic to cologne but insisted on sniffing him and her head blew up to twice its size.

"And I've got another modeling job next week," he told me. "A catalog. So things are looking up for both of us. What are you doing for New Year's?"

I had never done anything for New Year's except babysit. This year Mrs. Maclaren was going to stay home, and so was I.

"I'm going to Tijuana for New Year's with the usual suspects to go dancing and you know," Cruz said. "How about you come with?"

"To Tijuana?"

"It's fun."

"I can't dance."

"I'll teach you," he said.

"Your friends wouldn't want me around." That was true. As far as his friends were concerned, I was invisible. They wouldn't appreciate me showing up for their party at a club in Tijuana on the biggest party night of the year.

"Sure they will. It'll just be Eric, Dana, John, Tiffany, Felicity, and Caden."

It gave me hives just thinking about it. "I don't know."

"You'll go."

"You have so many friends," I said.

Cruz smiled. "That's a good thing, Tess."

"Okay," I muttered.

He cupped his ear with his hand. "What was that?"

"I said okay."

"You'll have a good time. I promise."

Yeah, right. I would have looked forward more to my own hanging.

"Not unless Webster changed the meaning of 'good time.' I still think you'd be happier with just your friends," I said. "You have so many of them. Who do you like the most? Eric?"

Cruz shrugged. "He's probably number three on the list."

"Dana?"

"I don't know. Number two, maybe."

"Who's your best friend out of all your friends?"

He raised an eyebrow and studied my face. "You are."

"What did you say?"

Cruz had beautiful eyes, but they were more than that. They were kind, gentle, a true reflection of his soul. He locked eyes with me and laid his hands on mine on the table.

"You're my best friend, Tess. Didn't you know that?"

I would have given anything for a good case of chicken pox or at least a broken leg. Anything not to go out with Cruz's model friends.

I had begged Cruz all week to let me out of my promise to go with him to Tijuana on New Year's, but he wouldn't take "no way" for an answer.

He kept saying I was going to have a good time. But I knew different. I was going to have a miserable time. The worst time. Joan of Arc had a better time being burned alive. I mean, at least she knew it would be over fast.

I, on the other hand, was faced with hours and hours with Cruz's stuck up model friends. At best, they would ignore me all night. At worst, well, worst could be pretty bad. I hoped they would ignore me.

I put on the dress Cruz had given me for my birthday and borrowed a pair of my mother's shoes that she had left behind. They were a little tight, but they were a lot more fashion model friendly than any of my shoes.

I brushed my hair, took a deep breath and one last look in the bathroom mirror.

"One last chance for chicken pox," I said. But nothing started to itch. I turned off the light and opened the door, jumping back in surprise to see Cruz's friend Dana standing there.

"Cruz asked me to see if you needed any help," she said as she studied her nails. They were black and pointy. I looked down at mine. No polish and cut short with a nasty hangnail on my thumb.

"Oh, thanks, but I'm done. All dressed," I said.

Dana scanned me from my feet to the top of my head. "You're going like that?" she asked.

"Uh, I guess so?"

She exhaled and rolled her eyes. She pushed me back into the bathroom and threw her bag on the counter.

"This is going to take some work," she said.

"Is it going to hurt?"

Dana and I were night and day different. She was wearing a skintight black micro-mini dress that barely covered her butt. I was wearing a flowy long dress. I was soft, slightly mushy. She was rail thin. Skeletor, Angelina Jolie kind of skinny. She had to be starving.

I wasn't starving. I had eaten two dozen chicken nuggets, a half of a box of Cheez Its, and two bags of Sour Patch Kids while I was babysitting earlier in the day.

Nervous eating.

But it didn't help.

I was still nervous. I almost ate the triplets' stash of Halloween chocolate, too, but I was already feeling like I was going to vomit.

Where Dana was sharp angles, I was round curves. Where she was tight mini, I was flowing long skirt. And where she was slick makeup and hairdo, I was sadly natural.

Dana was determined to change that.

She carried a whole arsenal of beauty products in her purse. She laid out a curling iron, brushes, and a Sephora amount of cosmetics on the counter.

"Oh, my," I said before she more or less attacked me with her stash.

"You look—" Cruz started and then shut his mouth when I finally came downstairs after Dana had finished with me.

I could have finished his sentence for him. I looked like a clown. I had an inch thick of makeup on. My lips looked twice as big as normal, and my eyes were hidden behind thick mascara, eyeliner, and eye shadow. Where was my face? Gone. You could have seen more through a burqa. Meanwhile, my hair was greased back to look—I assumed—sophisticated, but I thought it made me look like I had had a bad accident with a deep fryer.

How did I look? Not like me.

"It wasn't easy," Dana told Cruz. "She needed an overhaul. You owe me. Big time."

Dana walked past us and out the front door. Eric and the others were waiting in the driveway, standing around like a Vanity Fair Hot in Hollywood cover.

"Sorry," Cruz mouthed to me and held the door open for me to walk out.

It was my first trip to Tijuana, my first time even out of San Diego. Beyond my dread of hanging out with the models, I felt a little tinge of excitement to be leaving the country.

Not that it was such a big deal. The border was only a twenty-minute drive from our house.

Cruz and I rode in his car while the others piled into Eric's Mercedes. Unfortunately, Cruz's car started right up on the first try and ran all the way to the Mexican border without breaking down.

Cruz didn't say a word during the trip. He was probably still in shock over my face.

I couldn't speak. I was too upset. I looked ridiculous, and I didn't want to spend the evening covered in a pound of makeup.

Besides, my mother's shoes were pinching my feet.

We followed the other car over the border and into the center of Tijuana. They planned on going to their usual haunts, several clubs in Tijuana they partied at for the past few months.

We parked in a parking lot and walked two blocks to the first club. By the time we got there, the backs of my shoes had dug into my ankles, making them bleed. I was in agony, and I didn't have any Band Aids. I was too embarrassed to ask one of the models if they had one among their beauty supplies. None of them was hobbling around in their heels. They all walked like they were on the runway and like their four-inch heels were more comfortable than Uggs.

Uggs. I would have given my right arm for a pair of Uggs instead of my mother's torture chamber shoes.

I made a mental note never to wear high heels again.

Never. Not even with a gun to my head, which I would have preferred over walking in the Abu Ghraib shoes.

It was a relief to finally sit down in the club. It was packed. The music was on full blast. We were seated at a large table by the dance floor, just the beautiful models and me.

Up until that point, nobody but Cruz had paid any attention to me. They had been busy talking amongst themselves about things I didn't understand: modeling, fashion, and sex.

"Would you like a margarita?" Cruz asked me, while they were ordering drinks.

I'd never drunk alcohol before except the sip of champagne at Dahlia's party. I was a little afraid of getting drunk.

"A margarita for the young lady," Eric said to the waiter before I could respond.

Cruz leaned over and spoke in my ear. "Are you okay?"

I nodded, but I was way out of my depth and counting down until the night would be over. The rest of them, including Cruz, seemed to be having a great time. The drinks arrived, and they knocked them back. My margarita was delicious, just like a slushy. I drank half of it in one gulp. So refreshing. I was glad Eric ordered it for me.

"Time to speed things up," Eric announced, and everyone finished off their drinks, me included.

Tiffany hopped up and twerked. "Let's go boogie at Tijuana Charlie's!"

They all seemed to like that idea and followed her out of the club. I stood up, too, but the room spun around, and I stumbled into another table.

"Whoa, are you all right?" Cruz asked me.

"I don't know. Is the room supposed to spin around like that?"

"Make a note: one margarita is too much for Tess."

I thought drunk people felt no pain, but in my case, the margarita didn't help with my feet at all. The three-block walk to the next club almost killed me. The shoes had worked their way deep into my skin, practically cutting my feet off at the ankles. On the bright side, being in terrible pain and having the world spin around, took my mind off of being totally out of my element.

The second club was wilder than the first. Half of our group went out onto the dance floor as soon as we entered and were swept up by admirers who ground against them while the music blared. The rest of us sat at a table with a half-moon booth. But they didn't sit for long. A woman asked Eric to dance, and he agreed, and Dana asked Cruz to dance, and he went with her after asking me if it was all right.

That's how I wound up alone at the table in the club in Tijuana. It seemed like the entire place was having fun. Everyone found a partner.

Except for me.

I counted in my head. One minute, two minutes. At least five minutes went by, alone at the table when an older man approached me.

"Would you like to dance?" he asked me.

I didn't want to dance. Certainly not with him and not in general. He looked like he was in his forties, and he leaned over the table like he was going to lie down on it.

"Come on, nobody else is dancing with you. Let's dance. I'll show you my moves," he insisted, tugging my hand.

My skin crawled. He creeped me out. I really didn't want him near me, let alone to dance with him.

I looked past him and saw Cruz on the dance floor, dancing with three girls at once. His pelvis was grinding against one and another was grinding against his butt.

"Okay," I told the old guy and let him take me out to the dance floor. He wrapped his arms around my waist and pulled me close, dancing with me like he wanted me to have his baby.

I didn't want to have his baby.

And I didn't know how to dance.

Oh, damn. I forgot I didn't know how to dance.

I stood like a lump of clay and let him move me around. I

closed my eyes and prayed the song would be over fast, but the songs never seemed to end. The DJ made them run into each other, one fluid mix. Did I mention that my feet hurt?

My feet hurt.

And the old guy was grossing me out.

And there was something in his pants, and I didn't think it was a pistol. Yikes. Enough was enough. I pushed him away, thanked him for the dance, and started to walk back to the table. But he didn't like that idea and yanked me back.

Now in addition to being dizzy, miserable, and in pain, I was scared.

"The lady doesn't want to dance anymore," a familiar voice said behind me. It was Cruz.

"The dance isn't over," the man said to him.

Cruz got in between us. "She's done." There was a moment between the two men where they didn't blink and a crackle of aggression passed through them. I was afraid that they were going to fight, but it lasted just a moment. The other man backed down, and Cruz took my hand and led me off the dance floor.

"I'm done, Cruz," I said. "I want to go home."

"I'll take you right now," he said.

Finally. It was like music to my ears.

He said goodbye to Eric, which was like saying goodbye to

the rest of them, and we walked outside. The fresh air felt wonderful. Even my feet didn't hurt as much.

"Thank you," I breathed.

"Are you disappointed we didn't make it to midnight?" It was eleven at night. We had only been in Tijuana for an hour, but it seemed like days.

"How about we pretend we did. Happy new year."

Cruz laughed. "Okay. Okay. I get the picture. Let's go."

I hobbled to the car, biting my lower lip and sending prayers to the heavens to ease the pain. We finally got to the parking lot, and I was never so glad to see an ugly, broken down car as I was that night.

I sat down and peeled the shoes off my wounded feet. "Oh my God," I moaned. "I didn't think I would make it."

"What's wrong?"

"My shoes. I earned a Purple Heart tonight. Look."

I showed him my bloody heels and the torn skin. He gasped, which made me feel better somehow.

"Yep. It's like *Saw* but scarier."

"I'm so sorry, Tess. I didn't know."

"Why did you think I was hobbling around like I was?"

"I thought you didn't know how to walk in heels."

He was right. I didn't know how to walk in heels, but that was beside the point.

"I was hobbling because I was being murdered," I said.

Cruz managed to start the car on the second try. "I'm sorry, Tess. How about I buy donuts on the way home?"

"That might make my feet feel better," I said, charitably.

We drove through the night. I was happy to be heading toward home. I was looking forward to a big dose of relaxation with no makeup or uncomfortable shoes. I was not a party girl. That was proven once and for all. What was the attraction of going to a loud club to be pawed by gross men and get drunk? I would much rather read a good book in my quiet bedroom.

Or riding in a car alone with Cruz. That was pretty awesome.

Then the awesome stopped. We were on a dark road, about halfway to the border crossing when we were pulled over by the Mexican police.

A police car with a siren and flashing lights rode our tail until Cruz parked the car on the side of the road and turned off the motor. "Whatever happens, don't say anything," he told me.

"What do you mean?"

Cruz rolled down his window. Two plainclothes cops approached on both sides of the car and looked inside. The one on my side smiled at me and made a kissing noise. The other one said something in Spanish to Cruz, and he got out of the car, closing the door behind him.

Fear crawled up my spine and made me shiver. The police didn't look like they took the motto "protect and serve" to heart. Even through the language barrier, I understood they had more nefarious plans than just a ticket.

The two policemen crowded Cruz, demanding something from him, but I didn't know what. Cruz spoke in Spanish back to them. It sounded like he was trying to reason with them, but they were getting angry. I didn't understand what they were saying, and I couldn't imagine what they were angry about. I didn't think we had been speeding, and Cruz had had only one drink, and that was over an hour ago.

I squinted into the darkness to better make them out. One of the police pushed Cruz, and he stumbled back. He said something and took his wallet out of his pocket. The cop took it, rifled through it, and threw it back at Cruz.

It went fast after that. The talking turned to shouting and pushing and then one of the police pulled a gun from his back and pointed it at Cruz.

Chapter 17

Unable are the loved to die, for love is immortality.

--Emily Dickinson

I screamed and jumped out of the car.

The other cop took his gun out and pointed it at Cruz too, who was talking very fast in Spanish, seeming to try to smooth the situation, but it wasn't working. The police continued to shout and wave their guns.

"Get back in the car!" Cruz yelled at me.

I turned back, and in that instant a gunshot rang out in the night. I turned around to see Cruz punching one of the cops and pushing the other. He grabbed hold of one of the guns and threw it. "Hurry!" he shouted at me. I fumbled with the car door, trying to open it. The police were on the ground, shouting and looking for the thrown gun.

I finally got in the car and closed my door. Cruz ran back and tried to start the car, but it wheezed and coughed and wouldn't turn over.

Have you ever had a near death experience? Maybe flying in an airplane through a thunderstorm? Perhaps narrowly getting hit by a car? Did you think you were really going to die?

Sitting in the car that refused to start with the two crooked cops nearby more than happy to shoot us, I was certain I was going to die. My life flashed in front of my eyes, just like they describe in books. I saw the lunch ladies at school, my empty cookie tin, and Cruz telling me I was his best friend over fifty-cent tacos at Jack in the Box. Then with the short movie of my life over, I wondered a second about death, if it would hurt, and if I would get a second chance at life like the Buddhists believe.

But Cruz had other ideas. "We're not going to die," he said, reading my mind and pulling on the car's choke. Suddenly, miraculously, the car started just as the police righted themselves, retrieved their guns, and were running back to our car.

Cruz's broken down car that he had gotten for free clack clack clacked down the dark road as fast as it could go. I held my breath, waiting for the sound of police sirens and gunfire. Cruz drove, never taking his eyes off the rearview mirror. His hands held onto the steering wheel in a death grip. Neither of us said a word until we saw the bright lights of the border crossing ahead of us and the safety it represented.

When we finally got on the other side of the border, Cruz's hands started to shake. I touched his arm, caressing it lightly.

"How about those donuts?" I asked, quietly. I thought sugar and caffeine would help calm our nerves, and they did. We drove to the donut shop near the house, and by the time each of us ate four donuts and drank a cup of coffee, we had stopped shaking and could talk again.

"Are you okay?" I asked.

"Are you okay?" he asked.

"They almost killed you."

"They wanted money. I gave them my wallet, but they thought I had more and was hiding it."

I took a sip of coffee. "More money? Didn't they see your car?"

The fluorescent lights crackled and pinged and made everything in the shop dingier than it already was. The floor was covered in linoleum that used to be white years ago. It had been left to crack and peel, a lot like the shop's metal chairs with ripped red vinyl upholstery, which rocked unsteady with their uneven legs.

Dingy.

Neglected.

We were the only ones in the shop, and the fluorescent lights made us look dingier too, or maybe that's just how we were: Neglected, torn, and uneven.

"Here," Cruz said and rubbed my cheek with a napkin. Gently, he wiped away the layers of makeup that Dana smeared on in an effort to make me fit in. He used napkin after napkin to get down to my face. "I've been wanting to do that since you walked downstairs looking like that. I hope you don't mind."

"Dana wanted to make me look glamorous."

"Dana wanted to make you look like her."

"Isn't that glamorous?"

"No, I like your face. I love your face."

Cruz's eyes filled with tears.

The lights crackled and pinged and revealed so much.

"I—" I started and then was quiet. My hand was on the table, and Cruz put his over mine. He caressed my palm with his thumb, and goose bumps sprouted all over my body. We stared at our hands, mine open for him, his holding mine, his thumb circling, circling the soft flesh.

We didn't look at each other. At least for me, I knew I couldn't look at him. The small connection from our hands had spread through my body, and I was sure he would be able to read everything in my face.

"Let's get out of here," Cruz said, his voice husky and deep. He stood up without letting go of my hand and walked me out to the car. He unlocked my door and nudged me until my back was against the car door and he was pressed up against me.

I stopped breathing. I stared at his chest, still unable to look him in the eye. He emanated heat in the cool night air, turning my insides into jelly. He kissed the top of my head.

"How are your feet?" he asked, his voice still an octave lower than normal.

"Better now that I'm barefoot." I had forgotten about my feet. Forgot I even had feet. I wasn't thinking clearly. The buzzing in my body was back, and it was very loud.

Cruz slipped his arms around my waist. I managed to look up at him, and our eyes locked. His were as big as saucers, wide open and curious, his focus squarely on me.

"I've never met a girl like you before."

That could have meant all kinds of things so I didn't ask him to elaborate.

"You're so smart, and funny, and beautiful."

I looked behind me.

"What are you doing?" he asked.

"I was just wondering who you were talking to."

"Very funny."

"I'm dizzy again."

"Me, too." He took a deep breath. "You're going to Paris. You have a great life ahead of you."

"You do, too."

"No, not like you. I can't give you what you can give yourself."

"I'm not asking anything from you, Cruz," I said. But I wanted to ask everything from him. Somehow, I found courage or perhaps I just went crazy, because I stood on my tiptoes and kissed him lightly on his lips. He flinched, as if he was shocked. But his shock didn't last. He returned my kiss like a starving man faced with a meal.

We kissed for a long time, our bodies pressed together, transported to another place where everything was happy, where there weren't problems, and I wasn't standing in the donut shop parking lot with bleeding bare feet.

I was blissful, wrapped in physical and emotional ecstasy, but terrible thoughts ran through my head. Thoughts that this wasn't real, that I didn't deserve it, that it wouldn't last.

I stepped back, breaking the kiss. Cruz was breathing hard, his face flushed with color and the unmistakable proof of his arousal.

"Take me home," I said.

We rode in silence. I ran my hand over my face to make sure I was still there and hadn't disappeared in a puff of desire.

We entered the dark house, and I waited in the entranceway while Cruz closed the front door behind us. As the door clicked closed, he took me into his arms and kissed me hard, his hands traveling down my back.

I was blind with wanting him. His hands were everywhere, fueling the fire. He kissed a trail down my neck and nuzzled my ear. I moaned. My hands had a mind of their own, slipping under his shirt and touching his hard chest.

He took my hand and walked me into the living room to the couch. He stripped off his shirt and kicked off his shoes. He was beautiful. Perfect.

"Why me?" I asked. "Why would you want to be with

me?"

He blinked. "You're my dream, Tess. My fantasy. I never thought you would be interested in me. You're out of my league. Don't you see that?"

"Are you crazy?"

He laughed. "You're the most beautiful girl I've ever met. I could die in your eyes."

Slowly, he unzipped my dress and pulled it over my head. I was embarrassed to have him see me in only my bra and panties, and I crossed my arms over my chest. He put his arms around me and hugged me.

"My beautiful Emily," he whispered in my ear.

I shivered. He laid me down on the couch, took off his pants, and lay on his side next to me. He caressed my arm and touched my breast.

"Oh my God," I breathed. He kissed me again, his fingers traveling down to my panties. I turned to liquid heat, my fear and embarrassment completely gone.

Cruz locked eyes with me and never wavered. There in his arms, our bodies touching, I understood everything. Nothing needed to be said. But Cruz said it, anyway.

"I love you, Tess."

After we kissed for a long time on the couch, we went upstairs and spent most of the rest of the night in my bed kissing, talking, and holding each other. In each other's arms, we were finally safe. Holding each other, we were far away from bills and shutoff notices, from sick friends and corrupt police.

"That first day when I met you, I was almost too shy to talk to you," Cruz said.

"No you weren't."

"I swear. I had never met anybody like you before."

"You make me sound like a freak."

"Yeah. A beautiful freak. That's my type. Didn't you know that?"

I punched him in the arm. "I thought your type was models. You've been involved with a lot of them."

"I don't know what you're talking about."

"You're the Taylor Swift of aspiring models."

"You mean award winning?"

"I mean you've dated everyone in Southern California."

Cruz tucked a strand of hair behind my ear. "I tried to get you out of my system."

"And the fight in the kitchen? Were you trying to get me out of your system then?" The memory of his rejection still hurt.

"You must follow your dreams, Tess. You have to make it to Paris. You're going to do great things. I don't want to hold you back. Do you understand?"

I didn't understand anything. Cruz yawned and covered us with the blanket. He held me in his arms, and his breathing slowed.

"You could go with me," I said, but he didn't hear me. He was already asleep.

I fell asleep, too, but I was awoken three hours later.

"What the hell is going on here!"

I jumped out of bed, as if my alarm had gone off full blast. But it wasn't my alarm.

"Mom," I said. "You're back."

Chapter 18

Morning without you is a dwindled dawn.

--Emily Dickinson

I stood in my room wearing only my bra and panties with my mouth wide open in surprise. Cruz was in my bed, sitting up ramrod straight, his six-pack on display along with a look of pure shock.

Shock. Surprise. Understatements of the year.

I would have been less surprised if Bigfoot had walked in the room. Or Prince Harry. Or a giant potato.

I had never thought I would see my mother again. I thought she had found a new life in Mexico with The Boyfriend. I had gotten used to the idea that I was on my own, got used to the day-to-day habit of survival.

And more than survival. There was Cruz. He had become part of my life. He was the living part and the survival part. He was the compass to keep me on track toward my dream.

My reality had changed. It was a non-mom reality.

But now my mother was standing in the doorway wearing white capris and a tank top. She looked tan and furious, and she had died her hair red.

"Isn't this cozy? Playing house? So this is what you've been up to!" she yelled.

"It's not what you think," I wailed, standing in my underwear.

"I leave you alone for a minute, and you hop into bed with the closest boy? In my house? How dare you!"

My mother was good at being angry. She did it better than anybody I knew. She was the Genghis Khan of motherhood, but I had never seen her quite as angry as she was that day when she finally returned home and found me in bed with Cruz.

"I thought I raised you better than to whore around town," she screeched.

Ironic, right? Was she going for the gold medal in hypocrisy?

"Hold up," Cruz said. "You abandoned her without any money for months, and now you waltz back in here and start screaming about her behavior?"

My mother marched into the room and wagged her finger in his face. "Listen punk, she's underage. So, unless you want me to call the cops you'll shut up."

"Nothing happened," I said. "He didn't do anything."

She looked me up and down, and I blushed. Humiliated. I grabbed a pair of jeans and a t-shirt and quickly got dressed.

"You, get out!" she yelled at Cruz. "You're not welcome here. I want you out of my house."

He shot me a look, trying to communicate something.

"Don't look at her," my mom yelled. "You're done with her. Do you hear me? I'll call the cops and have your ass in jail so fast your head will spin."

"Is my father downstairs?" he asked. I could tell he was trying to hold his temper. He gripped fistfuls of the sheet, and his body shook.

"I don't know where you father is. I got rid of him. He was a supreme waste of my time."

So that's why she finally came back, I thought. The Boyfriend dumped her or she ran out of money.

"Are you planning on staying?" Cruz asked her.

"I don't answer to you. You're a loser like your father. Get the hell out of my house, or I'll make sure you spend twenty years in prison for statutory rape. Don't tempt me. I'm pissed at your family."

Cruz left the room, and I ran after him, sidestepping my mother. I caught up to him in his room and closed the door behind us.

"Don't go," I said.

"You heard her. I have to."

"She's full of it. She's probably just going to get the rest of her things and head back to Mexico."

But I knew that wasn't true. My mother had come back home for good. She had the stink of being dumped all over her—dumped by Cruz's father–and she would call the police on Cruz without thinking twice about it.

"She's here to stay," Cruz said. "And I need to get out of here before I cause trouble for you."

"Let me come with you."

"No. You're going to stay here and get your scholarship, graduate, and go to Paris. You can make this happen."

He got dressed and threw his clothes into a duffel bag.

"I can't do it without you," I said, my voice choking with emotion. "I need you with me. Please don't go. Please."

Cruz clutched my shoulders. "I won't be far. I'll stay at Eric's. I'll check in. I promise."

"But—"

"Nothing's changed, Tess. Nothing. Do you understand me?"

I didn't understand. From where I was standing, it looked like everything had changed. Cruz was leaving. Out of my life. This was a reality I couldn't face, couldn't live through. The pain was too great. It was like having a leg severed without anesthesia. No, it was worse. Every bit of happiness and hope was being sucked out of my life. A punishment, it seemed, for breathing. And loving.

He stared into my eyes, and my tears began to flow.

"Beautiful, Tess."

He kissed me tenderly, a feather light kiss that sent shivers up and down my body. I didn't want it to stop, but it only lasted a moment. He pulled away, and I watched him pack his bag. A minute later, he moved on to the bathroom to pack up his shampoo and soap. "Everything's going to change," I said. "Everything."

He swung his duffel bag over his shoulder and held my hand as he went downstairs. At the door, he took me in his arms, hugging me as if it was our final goodbye. "Nothing's changed," he whispered in my ear. "I'll be in touch."

Then, he left. I heard his car start on the second try and clack clacked down the street.

It was like a death. Like an irretrievable loss. My heart was crushed under the weight of it.

The house was quiet. Changed. One minute it was Cruz's and my refuge against a scary world, and in the next minute it was altered, a prison under the wardenship of my cruel mother.

"Where the hell is my TV!" she shouted from upstairs.

Selling the televisions was only the beginning of a long list of the things I had done wrong in her absence. She didn't offer an explanation about why she came back. She didn't offer an apology for leaving me and stealing my money. But she did offer a boatload of criticisms regarding Cruz, the house, and my party dress, which she found in a crumpled ball on the couch.

"What the hell went on here while I was gone?" she demanded, holding up my dress.

"Nothing! Nothing happened," I said. Nothing the way she thought.

No slide into home.

No condom needed.

White wedding dress all the way.

We had kissed and touched and held each other. Drunk with passion, overwhelmed with love, I would have gone to any length to prove my devotion to him and to please him in whatever way I could. But he didn't push me to go further than I was ready to go.

Content to lie in each other's arms, the night sealed our feelings and our commitment. At least I thought it did, but now he was gone, and I didn't know when I would see him again.

"Bullshit nothing happened," my mother said, tossing my dress in the corner. "Look at this place. Look at this dump."

I looked around. Besides our dirty clothes on the couch, the house was clean. But it was better not to argue with my mother. I had seventeen years of experience dealing with her, and it was always better to duck and weave instead of hitting her straight on.

Although I would have loved to hit her straight on and never stop.

Standing there in the living room, watching her march around on her high horse as if she hadn't abandoned me and left me with no money to fend for myself with the rent past due and no way to contact her, gave me a whole slew of murderous thoughts. I was fantasizing about all the ways to kill her.

Decapitation was coming at a close second to drowning.

I was hurting on so many levels, but I had to push that away and think clearly. I had to make a plan. That's what survivors do. They swallow their hurt and make a plan.

They survive.

As my mother threw open cabinets and screamed at me for not keeping the kitchen stocked, I took stock of my situation. There were six more months of school. With her paying the bills, I could make enough money babysitting to pay for my plane ticket to Paris and have a little left over. I would just have to find a better hiding place for my cash.

The other upside to her being home was she could fill out the paperwork for my student visa. It would be a challenge to get her to do it, to go to the consulate with me and jump through the bureaucratic hoops, but maybe just maybe if I was sweetness and light, in a moment of weakness she would agree to do it.

So I didn't kill her, and I didn't yell back, and I took all her punishment, every last bit of it.

She took a prescription bottle out of her purse and popped two pills in her mouth.

"The first thing to do is get a television," she said. "I'm going to lie down, if you haven't sold my bed."

Cruz was sort of right about nothing changing. For Mom and me, nothing had changed. We settled right back into our old lives like nothing had ever happened. She got her job back. Her car reappeared, somehow, and I didn't ask her where it had been. There was food in the kitchen again, and two new televisions were delivered one day after school. Even though she didn't come home with money, my mom had credit cards, and she was making good use of them.

During the first two weeks that she was back, she went through at least three guys. They were all much younger than her and none of them were ever seen again after one night. She seemed to give up on the whole happy family thing. She didn't force me to meet her boyfriends. In fact, she didn't get angry when I would run upstairs to my room as soon as they walked through the front door. That was a change. Before Mexico, she would always insist that I meet her boyfriends, as if she needed my approval. Also different was that she went out a lot instead of having parties at the house.

But the biggest change was the pills.

As far as I could tell, there were two prescription bottles that she used on a regular basis. In the morning when I would bring her her coffee, they were on her nightstand, and before I left her room and she would get out of bed, she would pop two pills in her mouth and swallow them down with the coffee.

She never let them out of her sight so I never got a chance to read the labels and find out what they were. But she was considerably more anxious than she used to be. Nervous. And after her pills, she would calm down.

After her initial tirade, she left me alone for the most part. I brought her morning coffee, cleaned up after myself, and didn't have a lot of interaction with her for the rest of the day.

No, she never talked about why she left, what happened when she was gone, or why she came back. But one day I found a new cell phone in my backpack, and I understood that that was some kind of apology from her.

The other stuff—the Cruz stuff—did change. He was wrong about that. He vanished without a trace. I didn't know how to contact him, didn't know Eric's number or where he lived. My energy level dropped, and even though I now had real food to eat, I lost my appetite. I made it to school and to babysitting, but I couldn't seem to rouse myself enough to do my homework or study. I couldn't even write in my notebooks.

Most evenings I sat by my bedroom window and looked out at the street, half waiting for Cruz to drive up. But he didn't. Once or twice, I thought I heard the *clack clack clack* of his car and ran out of the house, but there was nobody there.

It was like I was having beautiful boy withdrawals. I wondered if meth addicts had it as hard. My body was heavy, and it was difficult for me to move my arms and legs. I had a low-level headache all the time, and I couldn't get enough sleep.

And I would cry. Did I mention the crying? I cried a lot.

January ended and February began. I started skipping school, complaining that I wasn't feeling well. Days turned into weeks of lying in bed and watching the dust float on the sun's rays filtering through my window.

I stopped eating. Stopped caring.

Don't get me wrong. I wasn't one of those girls who believed Cinderella needed Prince Charming to make her happy. I was more of a Gloria Steinem kind of girl than a Millionaire Matchmaker kind of girl. I thought Cinderella could have been perfectly happy renting a small apartment in the kingdom with a couple of mice roommates and a job singing with birds or something. Sure, she could go out on the weekends with the prince, but I didn't think she *needed* him to save her and make her happy.

True, Cruz had more than a passing resemblance to Prince Charming minus the blond hair. True, he was beautiful, he knew how to dance, and he had saved me, but I was still surprised that I felt like I was dying without him.

He had changed me, made me whole. And now that he was gone, so was a big chunk of me. I was left with only half a heart, unbeating and useless. No wonder cardiologists made so much money. It's damned hard to fix a broken heart.

My mother yelled at me the first couple of days to get out of bed but gave up after that. I had stopped listening to her, anyway. I was stuck in a world where time passed in an otherworldly haze without purpose. Slowly the hours and days passed, and I half-lived them, unable to reboot myself.

Unable to become whole again without Cruz.

Maybe I couldn't be whole again because I didn't see a need to be, didn't see much purpose in doing much of anything. So I didn't, except to stumble into the bathroom when I absolutely had to.

That's what I was doing the week after Daylight Savings ushered in the spring. I closed the bathroom door behind me and locked it. I noticed for the first time in a long time after not noticing anything for so long that the bathroom wasn't as tidy as usual. There was toothpaste splattered in the sink, spots on the mirror, and two towels on the floor.

I jumped back, as if I had gotten an electrical shock. I bent down and picked up the towels and put them on the rod just like I had done almost every day when Cruz lived with me.

Cruz.

Something in me snapped. My apathy turned to a fierce need for action. I ran out of the bathroom, threw on jeans and a t-shirt, grabbed my purse, and sprinted outside. I took the bus at the corner and didn't sit down the whole ride to Neiman Marcus.

Gone were the Christmas decorations, but the rest was the same. Overpriced skinny clothes were sparsely laid out, like each garment was a work of art or a prize. I was no longer intimidated by the wealth and glamour of the place. I was singularly focused on finding Cruz.

I ignored the snooty salesladies and made a beeline to the men's cologne counter. The manager was organizing the glass bottles. She was still dressed all in black. Her face didn't move, her lips were blood red, and her long blond hair fell down her back in a silky wave.

I slapped my hands down on the counter. "Where is he?" I demanded.

She arched a perfectly plucked eyebrow. "Excuse me? May I help you?" She spoke slowly and said "help" like she had a totally different definition of the word, like how dare I talk to her wearing baggy jeans and a t-shirt with wild un-brushed hair and a dirty face.

"Cruz!" I said too loudly. "Where is he? I need to see him!"

"And you are?"

"I want to see Cruz!"

"I think we've established that. Who are you that you want to see Cruz?"

"I'm Tess." My traitorous tear ducts started working overtime sending tears streaming down my face and making my nose run.

"*You're* Tess? No, you can't be. This is too much." She laughed while I cried.

"Do you know me?"

"Honey, you're famous here."

I wiped my nose on my sleeve. "I am?"

"Cruz isn't here."

"I can wait for him," I said.

"You don't understand. He's never coming back. Never. And good riddance to him."

"He quit?" I asked. Why would he quit? He needed his job. How would he survive without it? Unless he left town. Unless he had decided to go to Japan early for his modeling. At the thought of him halfway around the world, my tear ducts revved into gear again.

"Not exactly. The boy suffers from bad judgment. Obviously," she added, gesturing up and down my body. "He had a freakout. Your name was mentioned."

"Freakout? My name?"

"He's obsessed or he thinks he's obsessed. What did you do to him? Drug him? Hypnotize him?"

"I didn't drug him or hypnotize him," I said. I thought she was teasing me, being a mean girl.

She shrugged. "Whatever you did, he has piss poor judgment. I'm a catch. Do you understand?"

"You're a catch," I repeated.

"And you're scaring away customers." She signaled to a

security man to come over.

"Wait. Where can I find him? Do you have contact information for him?"

"I can't give out private employee information."

"Please!" I shouted. "I need to see him!"

"He was fired, don't you get it?" she hissed. "He went nuts, went off on me, kept shouting about you."

"I don't understand," I said. The security guard grabbed my upper arm and squeezed tight. "Ow!" I tried to pull away, but he squeezed tighter. He dragged me away from the men's cologne department toward the exit. He was incredibly strong, and despite my determination, I couldn't fight him.

"Don't make this difficult," he growled.

I didn't know if I was making things difficult, but they were difficult enough. My trip to Neiman Marcus didn't get me any closer to Cruz. I couldn't find him, couldn't get in touch with him. All I knew was that he got fired, but I didn't know why. Because of poor judgment? Because of me?

My head swam with guesses, assumptions, and wishes. I tried to psychically connect with Cruz, to read his mind from afar. My thoughts swarmed, trying to figure out where he was, how he was, and how he felt about me. The more I thought, the less I knew, my thoughts only adding to my depression.

I was at a dead end. And as the saying goes, the only way was up.

Now that I had finally gotten out of bed, I did my best to show up for life again. I made "fake it 'til you make it" my new motto. I took a shower and washed my hair. I also did my homework. My appetite hadn't come back, but at least I was going to school. Mrs. Landes, the college advisor, heard of my return and called me into her office. It was the end of the day, and she wasn't her usual chipper self.

"Time is ticking away," she told me. "We're approaching the deadline. Have you gotten your paperwork filled out?"

I had all but forgotten about Paris. My mind was full of sorrow and longing, and there wasn't room for anything else like dreams or plans. Paris used to be important to me, but now I couldn't focus on anything except loss.

"You do still want to go to the Sorbonne, right?" Mrs. Landes asked. "I'm not going through all this bother for nothing?"

Did I still want to go to Paris? With Cruz gone and my mother in the house, I did want to get as far away as possible. Before I had wanted to get to Paris at all costs, but now I just wanted to escape San Diego at all costs. I guessed Paris was as good a place as any to run away to.

I nodded. "Yes."

"Good. Then, you need to get cracking on that paperwork. Take a trip to the French consulate in Los Angeles and have them stamp everything good and official. Okay?"

I nodded. I felt a tear threaten to run down my cheek, and I turned away to wipe my eye. Mrs. Landes touched my knee.

"I didn't bring you here just to get on your case. I have some good news." Her saggy face turned up into a smile. "Really good news. You've been accepted to the Sorbonne. I called them this morning to see what's what, and that's what's what! You're in, Tess. You're going to the Sorbonne."

"I'm what?"

"Do you want me to say it in French?"

"I was accepted?"

"I think I have a French English dictionary here somewhere. Come on, tell me you're happy."

I tried to be happy for Mrs. Landes. She had helped make my dream come true, and I should be happy.

Damn it, be happy Tess, I thought.

I tried to squeeze out some happiness, but I couldn't make it happen. I had been sad for so long that that had become my go to emotion.

"Of course I'm happy," I lied. I smiled to prove it.

"Good. Now go off, dance the can-can, eat a croissant, and get the paperwork done. Your dream just came true, and it's a mighty fine dream. I'm so tired of Ivy League I could puke. This was my first Sorbonne student application in 30 years of doing this job. I'm thrilled for you."

Mrs. Landes was thrilled for me, and I knew I should be, too. Thrilled. Happy. I wondered when the emotion would kick in or if my dream would be forever tainted by the sadness I felt over Cruz.

School was over for the day. I left Mrs. Landes' office and trudged across the empty campus on my way home. I had lost weight in the past couple of months, and my pants drooped as I walked. I yanked them up as I turned the corner onto my street, and that's when I heard it.

Clack, clack, clack.

Chapter 19

To love is so startling it leaves little time for anything else.

--Emily Dickinson

I ran full out down the street. Cruz's car had backed out of my driveway and was driving in the opposite direction away from me. I waved my hands in the air as I ran.

"Cruz! Cruz!" I shouted.

I prayed that his car would break down so I could catch up. His tailpipe belched black smoke, and I thought there was a pretty good chance it wouldn't make it to the end of the block, but his free car had a certain stubborn streak, and it kept clack, clack, clacking out of sight.

I stormed into the house to see if Cruz left me any message, any clue. I threw the front door open and bolted inside only to run head on into my mother.

She was wearing white short shorts and a push up bikini top. She was holding a drink in her hand, which spilled when I ran into her.

"What the hell!" she shouted.

"He was here? What did he say? Did he leave me a note?"

"Who?" she asked and then there was a look of realization on her face. "Oh…"

"Did he leave a phone number? An address?"

"Wouldn't you like to know," she sneered.

I pushed her aside and ran into the living room. I searched for a note from him, rummaging through the papers and magazines on the coffee table and on the kitchen counter.

"What do you think he left for you?" my mother asked, sauntering into the kitchen. She poured herself another drink and took a long sip. "A love letter? You think you opened your legs for him and now he loves you?"

I saw red. "I didn't open my legs for him. That's your specialty," I said, my voice low and cold.

The room got deathly quiet. I could see the words come out of my mouth and travel through the air on tiny molecules, the speed of sound turned ominously slow. When they finally reached my mother, they hit with surprising force. Her usual smug face turned to shock, the victim of the worst kind of hurt: truth.

But her shock only lasted the briefest of moments. She moved on to anger in a heartbeat. Her face became more animal than human. Predator.

She put her drink down and slowly walked toward me. I was frozen in place, unable to move. Without saying a word, she pulled her hand back and let it go, landing on my face with a terrible crack that made my teeth rattle.. I stumbled backward. My own hand flew to my cheek to subdue the stinging pain.

"Don't ever speak to me that way. You have respect for me, do you hear?" Mom shouted.

"Never," I said between clenched teeth. "I'll never have respect for you. Respect is earned. You're nowhere close."

I sidestepped her and headed for the staircase. She followed on my heels, and I could smell her liquor breath wafting from behind me.

"You think it's been so easy being your mother?"

"Is that what you've been?" I asked without turning around.

I took the steps two at a time. I couldn't shake the belief that Cruz had left me a note, some way to contact him. There was a chance he left it somewhere in my room, and I was determined to find it.

"That's right. Blame the mother," she said, marching up the stairs behind me. "Never mind the moody, ungrateful daughter. Always with your head in books or those stupid, worthless notebooks of yours. Scribble. Scribble. Worthless!"

I tried to tune her out, focusing instead on my room. While she threw insults at me, I rifled through the papers on my desk.

"I've done it all on my own. I never had help from anybody," she continued. "Alone. Making a living and giving everything to my creepy, loner daughter. You never lifted a finger to help me. You never once said, thank you."

She grabbed me by the shoulders and turned me to face her. "You're an ungrateful bitch, you know that?" she said.

"Nothing you say can hurt me," I said, cool as a cucumber. "I don't care about you. I've moved on." I pulled away from her and continued looking for a note.

"You moved on, huh?" she said and left the room.

My breath hitched, and I plopped onto my bed. I started to shake. It was the first time that I had stood up to my mother. I wasn't sure where my courage had come from, but I suspected it came from the total sense of loss that I felt. I mean, what more could I lose?

Just when I thought our confrontation was over, she walked back into my bedroom holding some papers. At first, I thought they were the note from Cruz that I had been searching for, but I recognized them almost immediately as something else.

"Where did you get that?" I asked, even though I knew she got them out of my backpack.

"Is this what you mean by moved on?" She smiled from ear to ear, like the conquering hero. Triumphant.

"Those aren't yours."

"I have news for you. This house is mine. Everything in this house is mine. Did you think you were going to hide this from me? Did you think you were actually going to make this happen?"

Did I actually think I was going to make it happen? I didn't know. But I hoped I would make it happen. I wished for it harder than I had wished for anything else…until Cruz entered my life.

"Let's see here," she continued, reading through the papers. "Application for student visa to France. France? You thought you were going to France?"

She cackled like a witch. "This is hysterical. Thanks for the laughs."

A seething anger built up inside me, ready to explode. "I got accepted to the Sorbonne. So, no. It's not funny."

"Who cares?" she said. "You might as well say you got accepted to a college on Mars. I'm not paying to send you halfway around the world to some hot shit school. Do you know how much that would cost?"

I knew exactly how much that would cost, of course. I had been running the numbers down to the last penny. It was doable now. And I was so close. With the scholarship, the Bergers' apartment, and my babysitting, it could happen.

"You're done with me?" she said. "You *need* me, kid. You're nothing and nowhere without me."

I bit my lower lip. I was tempted to tell her about the apartment, about just how much I didn't need her. But it was important not to give her too many details. Knowledge was dangerous in her hands. She would use it against me and sabotage my efforts.

"I wasn't going to ask you to pay for anything. I just need you to go with me to the consulate in L.A. and sign the papers."

"Yeah, right." She left the room, and I heard her walk down the stairs. I took a couple deep breaths sitting on my bed before gathering the courage to catch up with her in the kitchen. I found her polishing off her drink at the counter.

"I promise," I said. "You don't need to do anything after the consulate. I'll do the rest. You'll never hear from me again."

She poured herself another drink. "Little Tess is all grown up, huh? You think you can go and have some fabulous, glamorous life? You think you're so special? You think you can go to Paris just because you want to? Do you know how many times I've been to Paris? I'll tell you. Big fat zero times. That's how many."

She took a big gulp of her drink and pulled a bag of chips out of the cabinet. "I've never been to Paris or anywhere in Europe," she said. "I've been nowhere. And you know why? Because I had to take care of *you*."

She pointed a chip at me and took a bite. "I never had designer clothes, never could keep a man. All because of you. You know what that's called? Sacrifice. Seventeen years of sacrifice and suffering all to make your life better. Well, now it's your turn. You're going to work some crap job and be miserable just like your mommy. Welcome to reality, little girl. And there ain't no Paris in reality, believe you me."

I held back the urge to jump across the counter and scratch

out her eyes. It was hard to tell if she was only trying to make me suffer in order to win the fight or if she really meant to block any happiness in my life. My suspicions were leaning toward the second option.

"I'm going anyway," I muttered. "So I won't go to the Sorbonne. I'll still get to Paris and stay as long as I can."

"Not if I have anything to say about it."

She picked up the papers and ripped them in half and then into quarters. I gasped, and I choked up with tears.

"It doesn't matter," I said more to myself than to her. "I don't need you. I managed just fine without you for four months."

"You mean with your boyfriend?"

"My boyfriend?"

"That's who you think he is, right? Your boyfriend? You think you got a dose of puppy love? You got to play house for a while and now you think the world is all sweetness and light?"

I didn't think the world was sweetness and light. I didn't think Cruz was my boyfriend. But the love part, well, the love part I believed down to my soul.

"Like mother like daughter," she said, taking a seat on the couch. "You have good taste, I'll give you that. I can see the attraction. I've gotten very close to Cruz, too. Intimately close."

"What do you mean?"

"What do you think I mean?"

I grew cold and rubbed my arms to keep away the chill. I didn't want to be there, anymore. I wished my mother never came back from Mexico. I wished I didn't speak English and couldn't understand a word she was saying.

"You're a liar," I said.

"Did you really think he came here to visit *you?"* she asked. She turned on the TV and changed it to *Real Housewives.* "Don't you think it's odd that your boyfriend hasn't come to visit you and then visits you when you're not here?"

"I was late."

"He stayed a little longer than usual," she said.

"You're a liar."

"Am I? Well, if I am, I'm a liar without cellulite. I take care of myself. Men want me. Why would he pick you when he could have me? Don't kid yourself, Tess. Cruz is mine, now. I traded his father in for a younger version."

"That's not true."

"It's true. Cruz and me are like this," she said, crossing her fingers.

Santa isn't real. Ditto the tooth fairy. Good things don't come to those who wait. Pretty isn't as pretty does. And one more thing: Perfect, beautiful boys don't love Mess Parker. As my mother would say, "welcome to reality."

I hated her. I never wanted to talk to her, again. Never

wanted to see her. Never wanted to hear her voice.

"I hope you die," I said. It was the worst thing I could think of. She wouldn't care if I hated her. She wouldn't believe me if I told her what a horrible person she was. But she wouldn't want to die. At least not while she still looked good in a bikini. "I hope you go to sleep and never wake up."

My mother raised her glass to me in a toast and took a swig. I turned on my heel and went to my room.

It was only four in the afternoon, but I went right to bed. Any energy and joy that remained in my body had been sucked out by my mother. I was beyond sad. I sank into a black hole and didn't wake up for seven hours.

My eyes flew open. I had been sleeping a dreamless sleep, like death itself. I hadn't even moved in my bed, was still in the same position I was in when I first fell asleep.

Then, something woke me. The house was quiet and dark, but I could feel a presence, as if I was being watched. I turned on the light. My room was empty, but I couldn't shake the feeling.

I got up and walked to the window. Pulling the curtain to the side, I peered outside. There, across the street leaning against his crappy, free car was Cruz. I rubbed my eyes. I had wished to see him for so long that I wasn't sure if he was real or not or if I was hallucinating or still asleep. But he looked just like I remembered: Beautiful. Sad. He was real, all right. I exhaled slowly, as if I had been holding my breath for hours, and maybe I had.

He noticed me at the window and straightened his posture, standing at attention. He crooked his hand, waving me over to him. I nodded and stepped back from the window, letting the curtain fall into place. I turned off the light and tiptoed down the hallway to close my mom's bedroom door. I could hear her snoring lightly, which meant she was sleeping soundly and wouldn't be up for hours.

I walked downstairs and opened the front door as quietly as I possibly could. I clicked it closed behind me, making sure not to make a sound.

Then I was running across the street, and I didn't stop until I was wrapped in Cruz's arms. He hugged me like he thought I would try to escape. Body against body, my head nestled against his chest, arms around his waist, my hands slipping under his shirt to touch the flesh of his back. He smelled of apples and sunlight, and I couldn't get enough.

We stayed like that for a long time, locked in an embrace, as if we had merged, becoming one person. If it was cold outside, there late at night standing in the street in my nightgown and bare feet, I didn't notice. It was a moment of such relief. In an instant, Cruz had filled the black void in my heart with happiness.

"I waited so long," I said.

"I know."

"You didn't come."

He was wearing gloves against the cold, and he took one off to put two fingers under my chin and tilted my head up. We locked eyes, and I shivered. "I did. I was here the day after your mother returned. She said she sent you off to your uncle in Montana for the rest of the school year. No phone number. No forwarding address."

"I don't have an uncle."

He smiled. "I wish I'd known that."

"I've been here the whole time."

"I figured that out today."

"I looked for you."

"That's how I figured it out. Someone from Neiman Marcus called me. That's how I knew you were still in San Diego."

"They wouldn't tell me where you were," I said. "I didn't have a phone number or an address."

Cruz tucked a strand of hair behind my ear. "I know."

"I was alone, and I couldn't find you, and my mother said—" My voice broke, and I began to cry. He was crying, too. His eyes filled with tears, which spilled out and ran down his face.

"What did she say?"

"She said that you…" I couldn't say the words. I didn't want to know the truth, even if it was only half true.

"Tess, tell me what she said."

"Tell me she lied," I said. "I need you tell me it's all a lie."

He clutched my shoulders. "What's a lie? Tell me."

"That you and her...That you—"

"Me and her what?"

I couldn't look him in the eye any longer. I hugged him, shutting my eyes and leaning my head against his chest. "She said you came to visit her because, you know, you like her. And you did things with her."

"I what?" There was a rumbling low in his chest that got louder until he was laughing.

"Shh! You'll wake her up," I said.

"Sorry but that's the funniest thing I've ever heard."

"Really? I didn't think it was funny at all."

"You didn't?" he asked. "I'm fooling around with your mother? That doesn't sound like a *Saturday Night Live* sketch to you?"

It sounded more like tragedy than comedy, but I was glad he found it funny. Glad that I was right about my mom being a liar.

"I would never ever—I can't even say it—with your mother. Never."

His laughter died down, and he held me tighter. I felt warm and safe in his arms.

"I never thought I would see you again," he choked. A tear

rolled down his cheek, and I wiped it off with my hand.

"Me neither. Sometimes I lay in bed and thought I heard your car."

"I drove by almost every day."

"Oh."

I thought back to the times I heard his car clacking down the street. If only I had run outside sooner, I wouldn't have had to go through months without him.

"You got fired?" I asked.

He nodded. "I was upset. I might have said some things to my boss that I shouldn't have."

"You think?" I snickered. And then I accidentally snorted, humiliating myself completely. "Oh, God. I didn't mean to do that. It just sort of slipped out," I said like an idiot.

But he wasn't listening, or he was good at pretending he wasn't listening. In any case, he was probably too busy kissing me to listen.

He took me by surprise, capturing my mouth, pressing his lips firmly against mine. I melted into him, my mouth opening, his tongue slipping inside. The world spun around. I didn't know up from down. I was disoriented. Lost. My senses were on overload. His smell, the feel of his hard body under my touch, the taste of him. I was overwhelmed by Cruz but didn't want it to stop.

His hands traveled down my back and cupped my butt, lifting me slightly and pulling me against him. He moaned and deepened the kiss. It lasted forever. Hours or days or months passed. I had no idea. Lost in his embrace, I also lost all notion of time.

We shared a hunger that couldn't be sated, an itch that couldn't be scratched. We kissed and kissed and kissed until my lips were chapped and I was gasping for breath.

"I don't want to lose you again," he said. He was the most beautiful person I had ever seen. His eyes were big, brown and went on forever. Deep. Fathomless. His face was flushed from the kiss. His jaw was chiseled, all angles and planes of perfect proportion. I trailed my fingertips along the stubble on his chin and the area above his lips. He shivered, and I shivered in response.

"I never want to lose you again," I said.

"Good. We'll write each other when you're in Paris and then after—" His voice trailed off, not explaining what he wanted us to do after Paris. He pursed his lips, as if he was trying to get the words out but he forgot how to speak English.

"I don't think we need to worry about Paris," I said. "My mom put the kibosh on that experiment."

"What?"

"She tore up the papers and said there was no way she would sign anything to help me go to France. No visa means no Paris, Cruz."

I shrugged like it was no big deal not to go to the Sorbonne and become a writer in Paris as I had dreamed of since I started dreaming. But it was a big deal, and I surprised myself with the hitch in my voice and the tears that rolled down my face.

"We'll find another way," Cruz said. "You're going to the Sorbonne. You're going to become a great writer. I know you will."

His confidence in me was absolute and unwavering. Cruz believed in me, believed that I was special.

"Maybe someday I'll go," I said. The reality that my dream had been thwarted hit me like a ton of bricks. Suddenly and hard without mercy. "I can still write in my notebooks here while you go to--."

I couldn't get the last word out because I was too choked up with emotion. I wasn't going to Paris. Cruz was going to Japan. I was stuck with my mother, who hated me even more than before.

"I'm probably not good enough to become a writer, anyway," I said. "Everyone wants to write a book, but there aren't a lot of good writers. I'm probably just fooling myself."

Cruz's eyebrows knit together, and he frowned. "Shut up," he said. "You're going all the way. Do you hear me? All the way. Straight to the top. Awards. Bestseller list. Do you understand? Never doubt yourself again. Never."

I nodded. I had been holding my breath, and I inhaled sharply. It was intoxicating to have someone believe in my dreams, to believe in me. It was my first experience of another having faith in me.

And it was Cruz. Cruz believed in me.

"I love you," I said. The words were heavy on my lips. I had never said them before, not to Cruz or anyone else. They were difficult to say. Scary. But they were the truest thing I had ever said.

He caressed my cheek. "Do you?"

"More than anything."

"No, don't love me more than anything. I don't deserve that."

I was about to tell him he was crazy. He deserved that and so much more. He deserved everything. But he put his finger to my lips and shh'd me. "It's late. I'll walk you in," he said.

"You're right. I have to get up early," I said. "I have to wake up my mother in the morning."

"You're still bringing her coffee in the morning, even with all this going on?"

"I have a heightened survival instinct."

"Me, too. May I stay with you for the night? I promise to leave before she wakes up. I just want to be with you."

"You have to ask?"

We were deathly quiet entering the house and climbing the stairs to my bedroom. We closed the door and slipped under my covers, lying like spoons against each other. He wrapped his arms around me and held me tight.

"If your mother would get out of your way, there would be no stopping you," he said. "You're practically an adult anyway. You could become an emancipated minor."

I had wanted to become an emancipated minor since I was ten. I had plotted out every strategy to get away from my mother.

"Wouldn't work," I said. "She would have to sign those papers, too, and there's no way she would, just to make me suffer. She wants me to be miserable like her. She told me so."

"There must be a way."

Cruz was an optimist, but I had known my mother way longer. I knew she was going to block me from going to Paris no matter what.

I wiggled against him. It was so comfortable lying in his arms. I was suddenly taken by sleep and yawned.

"I wish it could be like this forever," I mumbled, half asleep already.

"It will be. No matter where we are we'll be together. Forever is composed of nows."

I woke up thirty minutes late. Cruz was gone, as he promised. I hadn't even heard him leave. I bolted out of bed and slipped into my clothes. I could still make it to school on time if I rushed.

The world looked a lot more beautiful after being reunited

with Cruz, despite my mother's refusal to allow me to go Paris. I was happy, even.

Being loved by someone made problems seem less terrible. In fact, I was feeling pretty good. It had to be the spooning afterglow. Why would anyone choose to sleep any other way? I figured that if spooning and kissing the most beautiful boy in the world was possible, maybe everything was possible. Maybe not only could I figure out a way to go to Paris, but maybe I could also bend forks with my mind and turn lead into gold.

What a wonderful world!

I whistled while I walked downstairs. I popped two Pop Tarts into the toaster and turned the coffee maker on. There was a little coffee left in the pot, and I dumped it out, pouring clean water in. When the Pop Tarts were done, I took a big bite and poured myself a glass of milk. I poured my mother's coffee in a mug and topped it with a little milk from my glass. I did a little dance in the kitchen and took the coffee up to her.

I had about five minutes before I had to leave, which was plenty of time. I opened her door slowly. Her room was bright for a change because the curtains were open. She must have forgotten to close them last night, I figured.

"Wakey, wakey," I sing-songed, still in a really good mood. "Here's your coffee."

I went to put her coffee on her nightstand, but there was already a cup there, half-filled.

"Did you already have your coffee?" I asked her. "Did you

make it yourself?"

She didn't answer me and didn't bother to move, which wasn't out of the ordinary. She wasn't what you'd call a morning person.

"Time to wake up," I whispered. "We're running late this morning."

I stepped back toward the door out of her range. She was ornery when she didn't want to wake up, but if I didn't make sure she was up before I left, she would make my life even more of a misery.

"Really, it's time to wake up!" I announced loudly.

Nothing.

No response. No movement. Not even the rise and fall of her chest from under the covers. Dead still.

"Mom?"

I watched her for a moment, waiting for any movement.

But there was no sign of life.

My eyes flicked to her nightstand with the bottles of pills and the half-empty coffee mug. A cold, icy dread rolled down my spine.

"Mom?"

I closed my eyes and listened. The room was quiet. There wasn't even a sound from the street. I willed her to shout at me, to say something nasty and threaten my happiness, just like normal.

But there was nothing.

I took a few steps forward and took hold of her foot through the covers, giving it a shake. Her head flopped to the side, but she didn't wake up. I stepped closer and leaned down over her face. She didn't stir and no air passed through her nose or mouth. Placing a finger on the side of her neck, I waited to feel a pulse.

Nothing.

Chapter 20

Tell the truth, but tell it slant.

--Emily Dickinson

I ran out of the room into the hallway. I stood with my back to the wall and shut my eyes, but I couldn't shake the image of my mother's lifeless form. She was changed, altered, her body abandoned by her soul or whatever that made her who she was.

I didn't know why I hadn't noticed before that she was gone. But looking at her it was obvious she had gone to heaven or hell or wherever dead people go, and all that was left was her empty shell of a body.

Dead.

My mother was dead.

"This can't be happening," I said to the empty hallway. "This isn't real." Mom had been in good shape. She never got sick. She wasn't old at all. How could she have died?

Crazy.

No way could it be happening.

It was so crazy that I began to doubt what I had seen.

Could I have been mistaken? Maybe she was fine. Maybe she was just drunk or took too many pills. Maybe I had felt for a pulse on the wrong place on her neck. I took a deep breath and peeked back into the room.

She was still lying in the same position. She hadn't moved.

Dead still.

"Mom?" I whispered, even though I knew she wouldn't answer.

The house was full of people, a hive of activity, everyone wearing uniforms and very focused on their jobs. A police officer told me to sit on the couch, and that's what I had been doing for an hour while they went upstairs to see Mom and do whatever to her and the house. From my seat, I could see a lot of picture taking and measuring going on.

"Would you like a glass of water?" a woman asked me. She was wearing a gray pantsuit and a gun holstered to her waistband.

I nodded. She filled up a glass in the kitchen and handed it to me back on the couch. She took a seat next to me.

"Aren't you going to drink it?" she asked.

"Huh?"

"The water."

I looked at the glass in my hand, unsure how it got there. "I don't know," I said.

"Okay, let me take that." She put it down on the coffee table and took a small pad of paper out of her pocket. "Give me your full name."

"Tess Parker."

"No middle name?"

"Nuh-uh."

"And you live here with your mother?"

"I—" I didn't know how to answer her question. Did I live there with my mother? What would happen now that she was dead? Where was I going to go?

"Nobody else lives here?"

"No."

"No boyfriends?"

I really looked at her for the first time. She was about my mother's age, around thirty-four years old. She had longish brown hair, pulled back in a ponytail like mine. She didn't wear jewelry except for a watch, and she didn't have any makeup on. She could have been me in seventeen years.

She stared at me as if she was trying to read my mind, and maybe she was. I didn't trust her. She was smiling, but she was definitely not my friend.

"Who are you?" I asked.

"Fair question. I'm Detective Stevenson."

"What's happening?"

"Tess, your mother has passed away," she said.

"I know that. I woke her up this morning. I mean, I tried to. That's how I found out."

"I was going to ask you about that. Why were you trying to wake her up?"

The image of her lying in bed flashed through my mind. I hugged myself and shut my eyes against the picture of her cold and unmoving. I had never seen death before. It wasn't like in the movies. It was final. It was the end. One minute the person you knew your whole life was there, and the next minute, they were gone forever.

"Tess?"

I opened my eyes. A middle-aged woman with a large purse and briefcase was leaning over, only inches from my face.

"I'm Diane. I'm a social worker with Family Services," she said.

"My mother's dead," I said and broke down in loud sobs.

"Oh, honey," she said and hugged me. She smelled good, doused in heavy, expensive perfume. She didn't let go until I stopped blubbering. She sat on the other side of me, making a law enforcement sandwich: the police on one side and Family Services on the other.

I was in a cloud, seeing the action around me through a fuzzy filter. I was ready for someone to tell me it was a mistake, that my mother was fine and that they were going to leave and let me get on with my life.

"Why were you waking her up?" Detective Stevenson asked me.

"She doesn't like alarm clocks. She wants me to bring her coffee in the morning."

"A second cup?"

"What? No. I mean, I guess so. It was her second cup. Normally, I wake her up and give her a cup."

"But there was another cup already there?" the detective asked.

"Yes."

"Are you sure?"

"Yes. It should still be upstairs next to…you know."

"Tell me about the pills," she said.

The pills on my mother's nightstand. "I don't know what they are."

"Was your mother upset? Depressed, maybe?" the social worked asked.

Upset? My mother was always upset, but as far as I knew, it was always directed at me. I had no idea how she was to other people. "No," I said. "She wasn't depressed."

I bit my lower lip. There was something about the pill bottles that morning that troubled me.

"She was taking heavy duty drugs," the social worker said. "Did you know that?"

"Heavy duty?"

"It looks like she took sixty pills this morning and washed them down with the coffee," the police officer said. "Do you know something about that?"

"I'm going to be sick," I said and ran to the bathroom. I locked myself in and turned on the tap. Watching the water run down the sink, I tried to think clearly. My mother was dead, killed by her own hands, swallowing fistfuls of pills with her morning coffee. She had gotten up early, walked downstairs, made a cup of coffee and returned to her room, slipped into bed and took the pills with a half cup of coffee.

I was crap at math, but I knew this story didn't add up.

Open, empty bottles. That's what bothered me, what I hadn't noticed before. She had never left them open before.

She also never made her own coffee. If for some reason I didn't make it, she would go to Starbucks. But she would go later. Much later. She wasn't an early riser, no matter how depressed she might have been, according to the social worker.

But there was an early riser in the house this morning. And he knew about the coffee, and he wanted to find a way to get my mother out of my way. In fact, he was determined to help me to get to Paris no matter what.

No matter what.

I rinsed my face off and patted it dry. The mirror reflected back the image of a grown woman, no longer just a girl. I had aged and matured overnight. Tragedy had aged me. With my first day as a grownup, I knew I had to push down my emotions and be smart. If the man I loved killed my mother, I had no idea how to handle it, but I wasn't going to handle it now.

"Don't say a word," I said to the mirror. "Don't say his name. Just put one foot in front of the other."

The social worker greeted me when I stepped out of the bathroom. Paramedics passed us on their way out of the house, wheeling a stretcher with a body bag on it.

My mother.

I stumbled backward, and the social worker put her arm around me. "Steady goes it," she said. "Would you like some water?"

"No, I'm okay."

We watched them wheel the stretcher out. When it was gone and out of sight, she asked me about my family. Was there anyone I could stay with?

No, I didn't have any family besides my mother. Dahlia

was in the hospital, and I didn't think the social worker would let me stay with Cruz on Eric's couch. Besides, I didn't want her to know about Cruz. I didn't want her to know that he knew how to make a cup of coffee.

So, I had to stay with a "nice family" the social worker knew until I turned eighteen.

"I'm going to Paris to study at the Sorbonne after graduation in June," I heard myself telling her. I took a deep breath. "So I need to be an emancipated minor."

"We can make that happen," she said, like it was the easiest thing in the world to do. I blinked in surprise, unsure if I heard her correctly. Somehow, within a few hours, Cruz's plan had worked. The obstacles were removed. I would be on my way to Paris in a couple of months.

She sent me upstairs to pack my things. Just like that, I had to say goodbye to the house I had grown up in to go where, I didn't know.

My room hadn't changed, as if it didn't know that the world had turned upside down and nothing would be the same again. It was still a girl's room, full of hope and boring routine. I was tempted to go to bed, put the covers over my head, and pretend the day hadn't happened. Just ignore the police, the social worker, and the zipped body bag with my mother inside.

Instead of hiding, though, I filled a trash bag with my clothes, making sure to pack Cruz's dress and Dahlia's hat. I dug my savings out of an old shoe, which had become my new hiding place since Mom had returned, and I stuffed the money at the bottom of my backpack, topping it with my school books.

Then came the hard decision: Which notebooks to take? There were way too many to carry. I rifled through them and picked out the four notebooks that I had filled since Cruz had come into my life. No matter what would happen, at least I would have my memories of him with me.

I was also concerned about the police officer's nosy quotient. It was probably pretty high. She reeked of suspicion and seemed not above reading a teenager's diary. I didn't want her to sniff around Cruz. I wasn't concerned about the questions she would ask him, but I was concerned about his answers.

I cleared out my bathroom and packed my toothbrush, toothpaste, shampoo, and soap in the trash bag along with the clothes. Then I opened my purse to make room for my lip gloss and perfume. Inside it, I found a piece of paper with a note scrawled in familiar handwriting.

My heart stopped. I crumpled the paper in my hand and listened at the door, sure that the police or the social worker would somehow know I had it. I listened for footsteps or even breathing on the other side of the door, but there was nothing except for the sound of them closing down the house. When I was sure the coast was clear, I sat on the floor with my back leaned up against the closed door.

Taking a deep breath, I slowly unfolded the paper. It was a short message.

"Everything's going to be all right, now. Call me when you

can. Love, Cruz."

And he included a phone number. I put it in my contacts on my cell phone and stuffed the paper deep inside my purse. What did "everything's going to be all right, now" mean? What had he done?

I was thinking of all the possibilities when there was a knock at the door. "I'm coming," I called. I gathered my belongings and opened the door. It was the cop instead of the social worker. Fear gripped me. I was sure she was going to arrest me.

"I thought I was going with the social worker," I croaked.

"In a minute. I just have a couple quick questions."

I was tempted to hit her with my backpack and run for my life, but I never could run very well. I could make it about a quarter mile before I needed to rest and drink a bottle of Gatorade.

"I feel like I'm going to throw up," I said, which wasn't a lie. I was having visions of spending the rest of my life in prison, which would be a lot like living with my mother but I would have to poop in front of other people, and my bed would be a lot less comfortable.

"Take deep breaths through your nose," she said, unsympathetic to my nausea. "Tess, I want you to talk to me about the coffee."

"She liked it with milk, no sugar," I said. I knew that wasn't what she was talking about, but I was trying to get her off track.

It didn't work.

"Why did you bring her a second cup of coffee? Did she ask for it?"

"I always brought her coffee in the morning," I said. "I didn't know it was her second cup."

"Was it normal for her to get up early, make a cup, and go back to bed?"

"No, and it wasn't normal for her to take sixty pills, either." I was sidestepping the question, trying again to get her off track. That time it worked. My logic was pretty solid. What was normal for a woman who took sixty pills? She nodded and put her notepad back in her pocket.

"Okay, Tess. Makes sense. I'm sorry for your loss. I'll be in contact if we have more questions."

She turned around as sweat dripped down my forehead into my eyes. I wiped it off on my sleeve before she could see the evidence of my guilt. I wasn't sure what exactly I was hiding from her, but at the very least I couldn't let her know about Cruz.

"Don't say his name," I whispered to myself. "One foot in front of the other."

The social worker took me to her office and filled out paperwork for hours. It turned out that a seventeen year old, newly made orphan was a complicated problem. There was a will to find, a bank account to close, belongings to sell or keep, and a mother to bury.

"We'll get you taken care of," Diane the social worker said. "It's a process. We just have to be a little patient."

"May I go to school tomorrow?"

"Of course, sweetie. Your life is going to be as normal as possible."

Hmmm…Normal. I wondered what that would be like.

Before we could get all the details worked out, I had to face my worst fear and get placed with a foster family right away. The social worker didn't lie about putting me with a nice family, though. Judy and Gerald Clarke were an incredibly nice couple, who were retired and more than happy to give their luxury guest room in their upscale house to a teenage orphan.

They fed me a dinner of steak and potatoes and were careful not to ask me too many questions, which was a good thing since the surprise had settled into shock, and I was having a hard time focusing and speaking.

I went to bed early. My new bedroom was clean and perfectly decorated except for my trash bag and beat up backpack. It was the home and family that I had always dreamed of. I sat on the bed and took my cell phone out of my purse.

It was time to talk to Cruz.

Chapter 21

Saying nothing ... sometimes says the most.

--Emily Dickinson

It turned out that my mother had a will, and even more surprising, I was her sole beneficiary.

"So you get it all," Diane the social worker told me in her office over a Subway sandwich lunch. "Which isn't much. Do you still want us to sell her belongings?"

"Yes," I said. I was never very sentimental about my mom's stuff before, but it still felt odd to get rid of it. I hadn't ever expected to be in this position. Suddenly, in her death, I was in charge of my mother's life. I didn't know what was appropriate to do and what wasn't.

Diane was helpful and patient, though. She walked me through the steps, with the ultimate goal to help me get to college in Paris.

"She had considerable debts, but with the life insurance policy from her work, she'll come out ahead. It will pay for her funeral and your ticket to Paris. About Paris—" she started.

We had been working at "the process" for a solid week.

For the first time in my life, I was asked for my opinion. Choices and decisions had become my bread and butter.

And Diane cared about my opinions and was efficient handling them. She put me on a fast-moving train towards my goals. All I had to do was "yes" or "no" at the right moment, and she got it done, which was a good thing because I couldn't get anything done on my own.

I was still in shock.

Paralyzed.

I didn't know if I was sad, exactly. Was I supposed to be sad? I hadn't had a Disney relationship with my mother. She hated me, and I wasn't her biggest fan. But she was gone and was never going to come back.

So there would never be a chance to have a Disney relationship with her. No new beginnings. No second chances.

Our last moments together were her lying to me about her sleeping with the boy I loved and me telling her I wished she would die.

And my wish came true.

My wish.

The reality of it hit me like a bomb going off in my psyche. I used a wish to make a terrible thing happen. How could I ever have the right to wish for anything again? Perhaps I was the bad guy in my life story and all my dreams and desires were wrong.

Maybe I had it wrong all this time: Perhaps my mother was Superman and I was Lex Luther. Perhaps she was Cinderella, and I was only the ugly stepsister.

Now she was gone forever, never to return, and I was alone with my guilt, which I could never talk about because it wasn't mine alone. I shared it with a beautiful, perfect boy. The boy I loved.

"It's not your fault," Detective Stevenson told me a few days after my mom died. I got a note in math class to go to the principal's office, and she was waiting for me there. She closed us in a room with a table, four metal chairs, and posters on the walls promoting reading and decrying the evils of drugs.

"I thought you would want to know," she continued. "Your mother crushed the pills into her coffee and drank it down. She didn't suffer. I wanted you to know that, too. She probably fell asleep a few minutes later and never woke up."

I gulped and tears stung my eyes. I doubted my mother crushed her pills into her drink instead of swallowing them like she normally did. It would take too much work, and besides, if she was trying to kill herself, why didn't she drink the whole cup instead of only half?

The police officer cocked her head to the side. "Sometimes they do it that way," she explained as if she had read my mind. "They crush up the pills and drink them down so it seems normal, like they're not really taking the pills. It was a sort of denial on her part to convince herself that she was just drinking her morning coffee. It doesn't make sense to us, but it probably made sense to her."

I wondered if it made sense to her, Cruz offering her coffee early in the morning. What did he say to her to explain why he was there? Did she even question why a good-looking man was in her room? She probably took the coffee with a smile, got halfway through the cup, and grew so sleepy that she decided to go back to sleep for a little while.

My tears flowed in earnest, and Detective Stevenson offered me a Kleenex. "And your fingerprints weren't on the coffee cup with the drugs," she added. "Just your mother's. Yours were on the other cup. So, you won't be seeing me anymore."

No fingerprints. I thought back to Cruz's gloves that cold night before my mother died.

Detective Stevenson got up to leave. "Tess, your mother was a very troubled woman. Depressed. She was taking serious drugs. Her coworkers and friends told me some doozy stories about her. She wasn't meant to stay long in this world. It was only a matter of time, and her time was now. That doesn't mean it's your time, though. Do you understand that? You've only begun to live."

I wiped my eyes. She patted my back and opened the door. "Have fun in Paris. I was there for a week back in college and had the time of my life."

And I never saw her again. The police file on my mother's death was closed, and she was free to be buried.

And I was free.

And Cruz was free.

"The school's college advisor has been more than helpful," the social worker continued in her office.

"Mrs. Landes," I said. Mrs. Landes had provided all the paperwork, and the social worker and I had traveled to Los Angeles to get the student visa. She decided to make a day of it, and while we were there we visited the La Brea tar pits and Grauman's Chinese Theater to put our feet in the stars' footprints.

Just like tourists on vacation.

It was all so easy. Every step of "the process" was seamless. Despite that, I couldn't drum up any excitement or enthusiasm.

"Yes, that's her," Diane said. "Mrs. Landes has locked down all the details on the Sorbonne. So that's done. I wrote a promissory note for the remainder of your year's tuition minus the scholarship. I'll send the check as soon as everything's paid off over here."

"I owe nothing?" I asked.

"Nothing. Doesn't that feel good? Your first year is locked and loaded, my dear. I spoke with the Bergers a couple of days ago, and your apartment is a go starting June first."

Easy. Seamless. Everything was falling into place. My life was going exactly as I had always wanted. But at what cost?

My mother's time had come and gone.

Dahlia was locked up in a hospital.

And Cruz?

That first night after it all happened I stared for an hour at his contact information, backlit on my cell phone. I didn't know what to say. I didn't know what to ask. I wanted to reverse time and freeze it. If only I could stay forever in his arms, lying like spoons.

Safe. Loved. Happy.

If only I never wanted to go to Paris and become a writer. If only Cruz hadn't loved me. If only. Then, this wouldn't be happening. I could be the hero again and not the villain.

He answered on the first ring.

"Are you okay? Where are you?" he asked.

"I'm in a foster home. They're nice people. The bed is soft."

There was a long silence, as we tried to figure out what way to take the conversation.

"Are you okay?" he asked, again.

"The foster family is nice. He's a retired computer programmer, and she used to design shoes. She said she would make me a pair."

"What happened? Why are you at a foster family?"

I cried silently, wiping my nose on my sleeve. "My mother died," I said. "She was dead this morning. I saw her dead body. I touched her."

My voice hitched. I put the phone down for a minute while I took a couple deep breaths.

"I'm sorry, Tess," he said. "Where are you? I'll come right over."

"No," I said, abruptly. "I'm going to sleep, and I don't think the foster parents would like that."

And I don't think I can look at you right now, I wanted to add. *And I don't think I can talk to you face to face. I don't want you to lie to me. I want to keep on loving you.*

"Okay, I'll pick you up tomorrow after school," he said, his voice low and comforting. "Are you going to school tomorrow?"

"I don't know," I lied. "I have to go. I can't talk anymore."

"Let me see you," he said. "Let me hold you."

"They're calling me. I have to go." I hung up and wrapped my arms around my middle because suddenly I had grown very cold. But quickly, I dialed him back. He answered on the first ring, again.

"Tess," he said.

"I love you," I whispered and hung up.

I didn't give him the chance to tell me that he loved me, too. I already knew he did. And loved me too much.

I also knew that he didn't ask how my mother died.

"It's the June first date we need to discuss," Diane, the social worker continued in her office. She handed me a cookie, and I took a bite.

"That's in four weeks, and I think we'll be done by then," she said. "I'm pretty organized when I have a fire under my butt."

"Thank you for helping me," I said.

"That's my job, cutie pie. I'm sorry you've had to go through this and need my services. But I have some good news, depending on how you look at it."

I held my breath. "Depending on how you look at it" didn't sound very promising.

"I've been talking with Mrs. Landes, and we figure you might not be all fired up about your graduation ceremony," she said.

I wasn't. I would be a party of one while everyone else would be swamped with friends and family.

"I was hoping to skip it, actually," I said.

"That's what we figured. It's not a big deal, anyway. Too many speeches and a used cap and gown. Blech, right?"

"Um, right."

"So, you're going to skip it because you won't be able to attend since you will already be in France."

"I will?"

"Yes, we've arranged with your teachers for you to take your finals two weeks early. You can graduate and be on the plane June first. No ceremony. How 'bout them apples?"

Them apples were perfect. My life was a neat package tied with a pretty bow. What I had always wanted had come to pass and in spades.

That's what I kept telling myself at my mother's funeral, trying to convince myself that my life was going as planned. It was a gorgeous day. Not a cloud in the sky, seventy-five degrees with a light wind blowing. The scent of orange blossoms and honeysuckle wafted through the cemetery. It was my first trip to a cemetery, and I was surprised at how nice it was. Peaceful.

A small gathering had come to pay their last respects or to keep me company. My mom's boss was there along with some of her coworkers. I recognized a few that had been in my house several times, drunk and partying. None of her boyfriends showed up, however, and I was sure she was pissed about that, wherever she was.

Diane the social worker, my foster parents, and Mrs. Maclaren showed up, however. They hovered over me like mother hens, making me squirm. Mrs. Maclaren seemed to be the most upset about my mother's death out of everyone.

When I told her about my mother's death, she had insisted that I come live with her. She said she would take care of me just like her own children. Even though I was touched at the offer, I thought she already had her hands full with the triplets. Besides, she wasn't an official foster family, and they wouldn't let me stay with her.

"I'm so sorry," she blubbered at the funeral, hugging the air out of me. "This is a terrible, terrible tragedy."

"But she's going to be fine," the social worker interrupted in her brightest Mary Poppins voice. "She's going to live and study in Paris. Her whole life is ahead of her, and it's going to be spectacular."

"Spectacular," I repeated with my biggest smile. It was the smile I kept using since my mother died to show that I was okay. It worked pretty well. I had almost convinced myself with it.

"Just remember to be precocious," Diane said. "Be precocious and the world is your oyster."

I nodded and kept smiling.

Then I saw him.

Standing just beyond our little crowd, dressed in a fitted black suit, his focus entirely on me. Cruz.

Chapter 22

Parting is all we know of heaven, and all we need of hell.

--Emily Dickinson

I walked slowly toward him. For the first time in weeks, my heart felt lighter. The trauma and upheaval that I had experienced washed away, unburdened merely by Cruz's presence. Our eyes locked and never wavered. I could read so much in his eyes, and I knew right then and there that even if I were the villain of my story, he would always be the hero.

No matter what he had done.

We connected without saying a word, our arms wrapped around each other in a silent embrace. My head rested on his chest, and I listened to his heartbeat to a regular rhythm, as if everything was all right with the world. As if life goes on.

"I want to leave. Will you take me?" I asked him.

"Should we okay it with them first?"

They let me go and even seemed relieved that I would be occupied for the day. Cruz's car choked and sputtered but finally started. We clack clacked to the beach, where we threw off our shoes and laid in the warm sand, facing each other.

He caressed my face, tracing a path from my forehead, around my eyes, down to my lips. "Beautiful Tess," he said.

"I—" I started but closed my mouth.

"What is it?"

"I'm so happy to see you," I said.

"Happy enough to smile?"

"No."

"Ah," he said, looking sad.

I kissed him lightly, and he returned the kiss, pulling me against him. His mouth was warm and sweet, full of love and caring. My body sprouted goose bumps. My insides melted. I longed for him even though I was already in his arms.

Would it always be like that, I wondered. Always the desperate need? The sense of belonging? I only wanted to be with him and nobody else. I made sense in his arms. Without him, I was only half, and maybe not even that much.

We kissed tenderly, the soft flesh of our lips caressing and exploring until we were so overwhelmed with emotion that we broke our connection, like a balloon untied and allowed to deflate in the wind.

I laid my head on his chest, and he rested his arms on my back. The rhythmic sound of the waves kept time with his heartbeats, as if the world decided to be in sync with us. As if everything was as it should be.

"I'm going to Paris June first," I said. "It's all set. I got into the school, and it's even paid for. I have ticket, a visa, and a place to stay."

"That's great, Tess. I'm so happy for you."

"Happy enough to smile?" I asked.

"No."

"Come with me."

"I wish I could."

"You can," I insisted. "Lots of models go to Paris."

He began to rub my back in little circles. "I'm just starting out," he said. "I don't have any work there. Besides, this is your adventure."

"I don't want an adventure. Emily Dickinson didn't have an adventure, and she turned out just fine."

"You're much more than Emily Dickinson, Tess. Emily Dickinson eats your dust."

"Yeah, right."

"You've just forgotten what your dreams are, but you'll remember again. Anyway, there's another reason I can't go to France. Eric came through for me, and I got a modeling contract in Japan. I'm leaving, too."

My heart sank into my stomach. I sat up straight and tried to breathe.

"That's wonderful," I said.

Cruz laughed. "Sure, that was convincing. You want to say that again with a little more feeling?"

"No, I really am happy for you. It's just that Japan is far away."

"We'll both have adventures and report back and then in a year we can be together again," he said like a question.

"Of course we will," I said. "A year isn't so long."

Not so long? It was longer than long. It was eternity long. It might as well have been a hundred years. Would he want to see me again after all that time? Would I ever be in his arms, again?

"A year isn't so long," he repeated, as if he was trying to convince himself. "Deal?"

I nodded.

The sun began to set, and Cruz walked me to his car. Sitting next to him with his eyes on the road, I finally gathered enough courage to ask him what I needed to know.

"What time did you get up the last morning we were together?"

"I don't remember. Maybe five. Why?"

"I didn't hear you."

"I'm stealth, baby," he said. "Like the wind."

He drove down the street toward the freeway onramp. The clacking was louder than ever. Drivers in the other cars shot nervous looks our way, worried probably that the free car was going to blow up or catch on fire.

"Did my mom hear you?"

"No."

"Did you have coffee before you left?" I asked.

He merged into traffic going south and didn't answer right away or for five minutes after.

"I don't drink coffee, Tess. You know that."

I did know that. He was a water drinker for the most part.

"My mother had coffee that morning," I said.

"What are you trying to say?"

I turned to look at him. His jaw was clenched tight, and his hands gripped onto the steering wheel like he was afraid it would fly away.

"I—" I started, but he cut me off.

"Don't think what you're thinking," he said. "Don't ask what you're asking. You'll break my heart and yours as well."

It wasn't any kind of an answer, but I didn't want to break his heart or mine, either. Mine was broken enough.

We were inseparable for the next two weeks. He picked me up every day at school and watched me do homework at the library or at Starbucks. He would be patient for a while but inevitably, he would play footsie with me under the table or caress my arm, which sent shock waves of happiness coursing through my veins and threw my focus completely off of school.

"My smart girlfriend," he said one afternoon. "Slumming with the high school dropout."

"Say girlfriend again."

"Girlfriend," he repeated. His eyes grew big and blacker than night. I flushed hot, and my stomach did flip-flops.

"Boyfriend," I said, experimenting with the word, letting it play on my lips.

We ate dinner together every evening and spent every last second in each other's company until my nine o'clock curfew. We talked about everything except one, and he tried to make it okay that we wouldn't see each other for a year.

I tried to remember every detail and memorize every square inch of him. I wrote endlessly about him in my notebooks, and he insisted that we take a hundred photos for us to keep during his travels.

A hundred photos and not one single good one of me. I wanted to delete all of them, but he wouldn't let me.

"Blech. I don't know what you see in me," I said.

"I see everything in you," he said. "You're lovely. Beautiful."

And then it was over. A week before I was to leave for Paris, Cruz left for Japan. I rode to the airport with him, Eric, and Dana in Eric's Mercedes. Cruz had managed to find a buyer for his free car.

"I hated to see it go," he told me during the ride to the airport. "But ten bucks is ten bucks."

We sat in the backseat, our hands interlocked and our eyes fixed on each other. I wanted to scream and cry. I wanted to force Eric to turn the car around.

"I can't," I said, choking on my tears, as we approached the airport.

His eyes had filled up, too. "You can," he said.

"No. It's impossible. Please, Cruz, don't let this happen."

"You're the strongest person I know. And the most beautiful. You're going to be fine. You're going to be happy. I swear it." He wiped my tears away with his thumb. "I can't wait to read your writing. I can't wait to hear you speak French."

We arrived at the departure terminal, and Eric parked at the sidewalk. Cruz said goodbye to Eric and Dana and got out of the car. I followed him. The trunk popped open, and he pulled out his suitcase.

"You are the love of my life, Tess Parker," he said, looking down at me, our bodies inches apart. "I've never met a woman like you before. You make me better. You make me worth something."

My tears flowed endlessly. "You're worth everything," I said. "I don't deserve you."

Cruz laughed. "That's the funniest thing I've ever heard. You're a riot. Oh, here. I almost forgot."

He took a box out of his backpack and handed it to me. I opened it. Stationery.

"It's embossed with your name. See? Gold raised lettering. I want regular letters from you, do you understand? Write to the modeling agency. They'll get them to me."

"And you'll write back?"

"And I'll write back if you don't mind misspelled words."

"I don't mind," I said.

"Do you mind if I kiss you here in front of everybody?"

It was a kiss to last a year. We melted into each other, desperate to hold on to a part of us, even though we would be so far away. Our tears flowed and mixed together, making the kiss salty and wet.

"Don't forget any of it," he said, finally, his voice wracked with emotion.

"I won't."

He took his suitcase and walked into the terminal without looking back. We never said goodbye, and maybe that was the way it should have been.

It was like holding my breath. That's how my life was after he was gone.

I passed my last week in San Diego, keeping busy with packing and memorizing the Paris Metro map. I counted down the days, living like the train in the story: "I think I can. I think I can," moving one foot in front of the other and breathing in and out as best as I could.

I took my final exams and said goodbye to Mrs. Landes. I paid a visit to Dahlia, but they wouldn't let me see her.

"Let her know I was here," I asked the nurse. "I'm going to Paris, but I'll write. Make sure she knows I'll write."

And then after the waiting--completely surprising me--the day arrived. It was my turn to go to the airport. Diane, the social worker, drove me all the way to LAX in her Ford and helped me with my suitcase.

"Be precocious!" she called out to me as I walked into the airport. It wasn't until I passed through security and sat at my gate with Paris CDG written on the sign above the door that I truly understood that I was on my way to Paris.

"My dream came true," I said to no one, a tingling of excitement bubbling up inside me.

I handed the ticket to the flight attendant and took my seat near the back of the plane. It was my first time on a plane, and I listened carefully to the instructions about the oxygen mask and the nearest exits.

"The first of a lot of firsts," I mumbled to myself.

After we took off, I opened my backpack and took out my most treasured possession. I laid a sheet of paper on my tray and began to write.

My dearest Cruz,

I'm flying above the clouds. I don't know what's ahead of me, but I feel you with me. Your love is my greatest gift. I'll never forget. I'll be forever yours.

Coming Soon

Don't miss *Forever Yours*, the second book in the Forever trilogy.

About the Author

Elise Sax worked as a journalist for fifteen years, mostly in Paris, France. She took a detour from journalism and became a private investigator before writing her first novel. She lives in Southern California with her two sons.

She loves to hear from her readers. Don't hesitate to contact her at elisesax@gmail.com, and sign up for her newsletter at http://elisesax.com/mailing-list.php to get notifications of new releases and sales.

EliseSax.com

https://www.facebook.com/ei.sax.9

@TheEliseSax

CPSIA information can be obtained
at www.ICGtesting.com
Printed in the USA
BVOW09s1504141216
470816BV00009BA/47/P

9 781505 635348